Ladies and Gentlemen,

May I present
to you ...

The Mandevilles'

MARVELOUS MARVELS

J. E. MILLER

Text copyright © 2021 by J.E. Miller
All rights reserved. No part of this publication may be reproduced in any form, stored in any retrieval system, or transmitted in any form by any means — electronic, mechanical, photocopy, recording, or otherwise — without written permission of the publisher.

This is a work of fiction. Names, characters, places, and incidents either are the product of the author's imagination or are used fictitiously, and any resemblance to actual persons, living or dead, business establishments, events, or locales is entirely coincidental.

www.jemillerbooks.com
@jemillerbooks

ISBN: 978-1-7374735-0-3

CONTENTS

PROLOGUE

I was born in the midst of a raging storm—both literally and figuratively. It was in the middle of the ocean that my parents found themselves with a pollywog eager to emerge. To debut, somehow, in the middle of a rugged wooden ship hull amongst the fluid swells of a sea filled with electricity and wonder.

On this night, a squall had crept up the ship's stern in an insidious fashion—as far as my parents were aware. The pair of them had been agonizing over whether this baby was reason to endure the juxtaposition of their plans, dreams, and personalities if they continued into marriage. This baby came as a bit of a surprise, or at least it wasn't quite planned.

In the lower deck quarters of a musty smelling traveler's den, the pain of the contractions began. As the waves crashed against the side of the ship, the groans and screams of my mother were mixed with the sounds of cracking lightning and the spray of the sea on the mast. My father watched in terror.

Dad was a wild card. A hard worker with broad shoulders and rough hands, a modest education but much creativity. My mother too came from humble beginnings. She was a black haired beauty with a pretty face and a reserved demeanor.

The two had found themselves young and in love, like many stories one hears. But unfortunately, my mother decided a lifetime with my father wasn't what she wanted. The revelation of these feelings came in an untimely fashion, but nevertheless a baby was coming.

A lady who looked to be in her early sixties was camped in quarters adjacent, and upon the unrelenting commotion she made her way to the source of my mother's cries.

"Sounds like you'll be needing some assistance," said a voice. "This old nurse hasn't quite lost her touch," she said as she walked up to the scene of my father's bulging eyes and my mother contorted on a bedroll. "My name's Margaret," she said.

Margaret, like my little family, was headed to rich Welmith Landing from poor Salturino for the promise of more sustainable employment. Trying times were pushing lots of families to leave their comfy home towns, pack up their most valued possessions, and move across the sea.

"You're gonna have to really push, honey," encouraged Margaret, "You're almost there." And all at once I was smacked with cold air, loud noises, and excruciating light. My father still says my first cries were louder than any lightning or thunder that storm gave us; a smile creeping across his face as he recounts it.

We made it through that storm and across the sea, but when I was very young my parent split. And I was always in limbo, not really sure which place or which parent to call home. When I was with her, I missed him. When I was with him, I missed her.

I spent years bouncing around between them and their clans. Their perspectives on life and the world as a whole were like night and day. I made up my own mind, some place in the middle, after squirming my way through opposing ideals. And somewhere in that time I met Whisper. At the time, I didn't quite understand just how much I would need them. I didn't know the journey that lay ahead of me. The struggle, the heartbreak. Somehow despite it, Whisper made sure I was no stranger to laughter, peace, and most of all love.

To know my childhood is to know what makes me who I am. It's why I say and feel the things I say and feel today. The life of a gypsy in search of the next adventure, a wanderer looking for the peaceful in between. Ever in search of reconciling the great divide I was born into. Always looking for home.

Chapter 1

The Train Ride

"Wake up, Janie," an urgent voice slowly intensified in my resting ear as if someone was turning the volume up on a radio. "We're about thirty minutes away from pulling into the station."

"Five more minutes," I stammered.

"You're gonna miss the best part," he countered. I lifted a heavy eyelid to squint at Alex.

This train's passenger compartments weren't the fanciest but had crimson seat cushions soft enough for me to curl up on. I needed to catch up on some sleep I had lost on my long and late night walk to meet Alex at the station. I glanced out the window to find we were rounding on a curve and approaching some dark wooden trestle. The deep green pasture land surrounding us was a breathtaking contrast against a perfectly clear blue sky. There were no clouds visible, only the trailing puffs of steam drifting up and out of the smoke box. We crossed the trestle above a wide river eagerly rushing underneath us, disregarding us above its surface. I felt not unlike that river, anxious to keep moving and avoiding looking around for too long. If you hesitate, you may change your mind. I had committed to something new, and I intended to stay on track.

"You're right," I said. "This is the best part."

I had never been on a train before and had always wanted to ride one since I was a little girl. My first ride would be a one way, but it didn't matter. I was on my own time now.

I had been traveling ever since I left home four years prior. I spent a couple years in Burnesburg where I studied anthropology and human movement on my parents' hard earned dime; but mainly sowed my wild oats. A year of partying multiple days a week starts to physically and mentally drain a person. I had a good time, but I began to realize that there was an empty place in my soul that needed to be filled with something more substantial and purposeful.

From there I headed to Dobbing Forge, where the community got to experience the seasons but winters were dreadful. Snow was not something I had grown up with, and in Dobbing Forge the skies were often gray with cloud cover. The energy level of the town, and consequently its inhabitants, seemed stuck in a daily repeating flatness. It made me feel like a rat in a wheel. Even so, the move was an upgrade as far as working on my health and mental well-being goes. I detoxed my liver and started picking up odd jobs to make ends meet. One needs money to cover groceries and rent; which was paid at a variety of apartment complexes that I moved in and out of every few months. Being the way I tend to be, it didn't take very long for the restlessness to rear its ugly head. Soon my eyes started to wander across a crumpled and faded old road map again.

After a while, I decided Espíritu Del Mar was the place for me and made plans to move south. There would be warm breezes, sandy shorelines, and the most beautiful teal green waters maybe on the whole planet. I thanked my employer for the opportunity and informed the landlord I was vacating the apartment. Packing everything I owned into two large and well worn suitcases, I felt that stir of excitement in my heart that occurs every time I scratch the itch to wander.

Thumb up and feet moving forward, I managed to catch a ride on three occasions to travel south to Espíritu Del Mar. The folks who drove me were kind hearted. They helped the time pass during our travel by telling me stories of their families and hometowns. Most of them were good listeners as I recounted my own stories, and they wished me luck when I heaved my suitcases over the truck bed or out of the trunk.

When I arrived in Espíritu Del Mar it was night, but it seemed like the whole seaside city was aglow. It was not a large city, but because it was spread along the shoreline, it felt like the biggest place I had ever been. The lights of stores and restaurants illuminated the road. Soft rainbows of color that beamed from street signs, in windows, and strung across old wooden patios where people dined or had cocktails provided a warm ambience. A dark silhouette of palm trees framed my view as the moon reflected off the smooth ripples of sea; which was nestled just a mere fifty yards away. A warm salty breeze brushed my cheeks, and I thought that was it for me. It felt magical.

It was in Espíritu Del Mar that I met Alex, in a local beach front restaurant and bar. He was hidden behind a drum set on stage, playing with a band he had been roaming the area with for the past six months. They were pretty good, but before I even met him I could see in his face that he wasn't content playing covers at beach bars.

At the end of their set, Alex's band started breaking down their equipment and making way for the next band scheduled to take the stage. He happened to crash onto the bar stool next to me after loading up his drum set. The following band exuded an entirely different impression with gimmicky costumes and vulgar diatribes, but they provided a conversation starter.

"Get a load of these clowns," I jerked a thumb towards the stage. Alex raised an eyebrow as he sipped from a glass.

"I don't know what you mean. These guys are always a hit with the ladies," Alex perked up a little.

"Their sound, and look for that matter, is quite different from your group. I thought you guys sounded pretty good." I didn't want to sound over eager.

"I guess it's more about the music for us," he half laughed. As Alex had finished his sentence, we watched the new band's lead singer squat down to get eye level with a girl about a third of his age. He brushed the girl's hair out of her face and winked at her before standing up and sauntering across the stage to the next one.

"Wow, you mean you don't try to pull any of these stunts?" I asked.

"No, but if I had more creative liberties with my band, I would incorporate real stunts to keep people's attention," he said as his eyes grew brighter. I wasn't sure what to make of that statement, but I was intrigued. We kept up the light chat and Alex started telling me about a project he had been working on that involved a moving drum platform. He said it would make for a real show, something people aren't used to seeing. I watched his face light up when he talked about engineering this contraption. I was drawn to a personality that could believe in the unknown and see the not yet devised.

I knew we would be great friends after we outran the angry bar owner who was attempting to kick us out for causing a ruckus whilst antagonizing the tawdry band onstage. After a drink I had grown more interactive and fancied a karaoke, but the band declined my request. Just as my old drinking habits used to go, I climbed onstage and grabbed the mic from the lead singer's wiry hand. I pulled on a strand of his long curly hair before turning to the audience and with the mock voice of a radio host asked, "Now, are these locks really yours or can I borrow this wig?" The singer lunged as Alex pulled me off stage by the waist and herded me toward the exit. We hopped in his car and laughed down the road until we hit the nearest diner still open. Bellies full, we talked all night about the big dreams we had. To spend our precious youth doing something exciting rather than falling in line with all the other people our age who were starting families and transforming into mindless worker drones for big companies.

I spent the next two years waiting tables at the same restaurant that Alex bar tended at. It was a monotonous day job, but in my spare time I started learning and practicing circus arts from a little place in town. I had seen the company perform at the square on Main Street during a holiday and thought it would be a fun work out if nothing else.

I was first introduced to the aerial world by way of silks. The apparatus was a long tricot fabric looped in and rigged to a swiveling attachment that hung from a beam in the ceiling. This created two flowing pieces of fabric that were used to climb and tie one's feet in. Once that was mastered, an aerialist could wrap into the silks in a variety of poses from splits and arabesques to upside down inversions and tumbling drops. It was like performing ballet in the air, and I quickly became utterly addicted. However, many practices were spent frustrated that my moves weren't fluid, my drops weren't graceful, and my endurance was far from the level I needed for climbing. Nevertheless, a year went by and I felt more steady.

Another year passed and conditioning had made my transitions of poses more natural. After all that hard work, I was more inclined to show off.

"Seeing the river makes me miss the ocean," I said while gazing out the window as we chugged over the trestle.

"We'll get back to the water one day. Keep your head in the game," Alex replied.

The *game* was a plan that Alex and I had hatched during our stent in Espíritu Del Mar, to travel city by city and cross the continents until we finally got to Fimaldi Hunu.

Fimaldi Hunu was a huge place that had everything, the best of all worlds. It had city life, full of opportunity, ever changing and progressing. And it also had areas of natural outskirts and coastal waters.

There Alex's drumming career would have maximum potential to take off. Plus his drumming role model, Shaun Hudson—whom he was obsessed with, had a studio there. As for me, I could explore a variety of career fields; since I was still trying to find my niche. If I did nothing there but spend fire lit evenings listening to Caribbean music, swim with colorful fish, bike carefree through the city, and enjoy amazing food and drink—that would be good enough for me. Alex and I were both convinced that if we could just get there, we'd be set. To us, Fimaldi Hunu was like Shangri-La.

Six months into the journey, we had been to three cities but were still very far from our goal destination. We worked temporary odd jobs until we had enough money to move to the next city. Occasionally Alex would get a drumming gig or I would perform for club ambiance. Those paid slightly better, but money was tight and definitely not coming in as quickly as we had hoped. Around the time summer was drawing to an end, we had enough to head to Aspirlington. It would be the biggest city we had stopped in yet.

"I've gotta hit the ladies' room," I said.

"Thanks for letting me know," Alex said, playfully rolling his eyes. I shot him an ugly face. I pulled open the sliding door of our compartment to a slender hallway on the left side of the train car.

As I looked out, I saw an affable gentleman further down the hallway walking in the same direction I was about to go. He wore a navy short-sleeve button-up shirt, dark gray pressed slacks, and a tan short-brimmed hat. He courteously nodded, and I gave a polite smile before stepping out in front of him and leading the way to the unisex facilities.

Evidently lots of passengers wanted to hit the head before we pulled into station. As we waited, the friendly gentleman stated, "Gorgeous view, huh?"

He was gesturing out the windows at the rolling green hills. "We have pasture land where I'm from but it's not as aesthetic as this," he said with a sigh and folded his hand under his chin.

"Same here," I replied. "Well, at least in my home town anyways," I added.

"You're a traveler?" he asked.

"Something like that," I replied. "What about you?"

"Entertainment industry. I'm actually here to audition for a show," he said with a smile and rising up on his toes a bit.

"Really? What kind of show?" I was intrigued.

"The Mandevilles' Marvelous Marvels," he replied.

"Sounds very enigmatic," I said as I turned more to face him.

"It is, actually. I hear that they're in the market to hire creative novelties. Pay decent money too, but it's the covered travel that piqued my interest," the man said with a raise of his eyebrows and a cheery grin.

"Are the auditions open to the public?" I asked.

"I believe so. They start tomorrow morning at nine o'clock."

"Where at?"

"The old theater on Third Street," he said a little more slowly. He was eyeing me with a bit more curiosity, but the line to the facilities had moved and I was next. I turned to take a step forward.

"My name's Zeke," the man said from behind me.

I turned around again and extended my hand, "Janie."

"Sounds like I might see you there?"

"You might," I replied as the cogs turned inside my head.

The bathroom door swung open and a pudgy lady squeezed past us. I half smiled at Zeke and stepped inside.

While washing up at the sink I made an appraisal of my appearance. Not much had changed over the last four years. Wavy brown hair, green eyes, and sandy skin tones in the mirror under the dim overhead light. Thinking about the prior conversation, a feeling bubbled up as I peered at my reflection. Like an odd happenstance or a kismet opportunity to make some changes or become something new. The gypsy lifestyle provided the option to frequently re-invent oneself. However, this time the feeling had a unique sense of exhilaration and expectation wrapped around it. It was brimming up as my pulse increased. I couldn't wait to impart the information I had just received to Alex. This could potentially be a gig.

I stepped out of the bathroom and nodded at Zeke as I walked back to my passenger compartment. When I slid open the door, Alex barely looked up from his Rolling Stone magazine.

"I've found us a gig," I beamed at him.

"Really?" His face still flat and unfazed. "While you were in the bathroom?"

"I met a man while I was waiting in line. He says there's a show that's taking auditions tomorrow. We should do it." I urged.

"What kind of show?" he asked with a look of apprehension.

Alex had been working resolutely to improve his drumming skills and showmanship since I met him. The rig that he had been more or less inventing was coming together. Like a scientist testing and re-testing hypotheses, he was very methodical and perfectionistic. Daily he hammered and cauterized metal, attaching pieces on and ripping pieces back off. The contraption was comprised of a platform on wheels, to which the drum set itself was welded and braced onto. The idea was to ensure that there was no way gravity could pry it loose. Next, Alex worked on creating a chair, rather than a swiveling stool, that would allow him enough movement and support to perform impressive trills, rolls, and double bass pedaling. He was now attempting to construct the grandest portion of the project; the track. His vision was that this track would include an ascending wave that would allow him to travel across the top of the crowd and a circular loop in which he could perform completely upside down.

"I know you are going to be particular about your debut, but hear me out," I pleaded. "This show apparently has an interest in routinely picking up new and unique acts."

"I don't know. I don't have a track. I don't even have the money to start building a track," he said with a gloomy look shifting across his face.

"What if they could fund you? Maybe it's worth going to the auditions just to show them what you've got and present the plan."

Alex wasn't overly eager. The track was going to take quite a bit of financing, but I could see the cogs turning in his head. It was no small effort to get the drum platform loaded into any sort of transportation vehicle, and it would be very difficult to get it to the auditions. But I pressed onward.

"I'm going to do a silks routine; hopefully they have a need for an aerialist. However, your invention is unprecedented. You are our selling point!" I smiled like a child begging its parents for a new puppy. "This could be a big break for both of us. We're already traveling anyway. Why not do it on someone else's dime? Plus get paid for it. It could take us all the way to Fimaldi Hunu."

He was thinking, staring blankly ahead.

As far as I had learned, Alex's upbringing was pretty normal. During his childhood he made good grades and stayed out of trouble, but he somehow developed a skill of analyzing the rules of safety and the dangers of risks at an early age. While risk analysis is not necessarily a bad thing, it made it challenging for a modern traveler to get along with sometimes. On top of that, Alex had not been well travelled prior to our little plan. He'd rarely gone anywhere outside of his hometown.

"I need more information. What is the name of the show? Do we know anything about the owners?"

"Well, maybe Zeke could fill us in," I replied eagerly.

"Who is Zeke?" he asked.

"Zeke is the man I met waiting in line. I can introduce you and we can spend the rest of the ride getting more information. He came from that direction," I gestured toward the right side of the hallway. "Come on, we've got about ten minutes," I said.

Alex rolled his eyes and slowly rose up to stand as I pulled on his sleeve. I slid open the compartment door and looked both ways along the hallway before stepping out. Walking along the narrow space, I could hear couples discussing their agendas and kids giggling as their parents instructed them to start picking up their toys. I glanced into each window, looking to find the nice young man in the felt hat. We had almost reached the end of the hallway. I looked over my shoulder at Alex, who had a questioning and annoyed look on his face, and peeked in the window of the last compartment door in the car.

It was Zeke. He was alone, seated on the bench, and bending over toward a carrier case on the floor beside him. The case was fairly large, maybe two by three feet, and had small holes patterned into stars along the top half of it. Though muffled through the sliding door, it sounded like Zeke was finishing a sentence.

I knocked gently on the window. Zeke quickly sat up straight, shifted his gaze to the door, and was up on his feet before I could wave in at him. He slid the door open just enough to where I could see his face.

"Janie," he smiled, though he looked surprised.

"Hi. I didn't mean to startle you. I know we just met, but I wanted to introduce you to my friend Alex. I've been telling him about the auditions."

Zeke nodded and shook Alex's hand.

"Alex, nice to meet you," Zeke said. "Listen, I would invite you guys in, but I've got to finish something up before we get to the station. Would you guys like to grab a coffee or something later on? I can tell you a little more about the Mandevilles."

"Oh, that would be so great," I said eagerly. "I'm trying to convince Alex to give this thing a shot with me. He's a musician; a unique one at that." I couldn't help but continue sporadically glancing toward the carrier case.

"A unique musician?" Zeke responded thoughtfully. "Very cool. How about Braxton's Black Brew at one-thirty?"

"We will see you there!" I replied, excited and feeling hopeful.

Zeke smiled, nodded, and slowly began to slide the door to. Just before it closed completely I could have sworn I saw a small dark hand wrap its fingers around a bar on the left side of the case.

Chapter 2

Braxton's Black Brew

Our train had met its destination in Aspirlington. The sun was still bright within a cloudless periwinkle sky. As the horn whistled, we decelerated into the station at a smooth rolling stop. Outside the window I could see the hustle and bustle of those milling about the terminal. A variety of faces, hopeful, apathetic, and anxious, crammed into the walkways.

Alex and I stepped down off the railway car. To lay eyes on the station was a catalyst for the butterflies in my stomach to wake up. It was a huge dome shaped building with sapphire blue glass, fading ombre at the peak of the arc. The magnificent curving ceiling sloped down and was edged with emerald and amethyst stained glass that led to the floor. The light filtering through those colored glass windows made the room grandiose. The two of us stared, mouths agape in surprise and wonder for what felt like several minutes. I couldn't help feeling inferior.

Unloading our paraphernalia from the train was no easy task due to the sheer brute strength it demanded. We pleaded for paid assistance to two construction workers who were passing through to the food court for their lunch break. The cost for their trouble required us to think even cheaper than usual when deciding on lunch. Later, we ended up settling on street hot dogs from a stubbly and miserable looking vendor. I wasn't sure how sanitary the steaming vat of smelly water they were pulled from was, but you cannot beat a two dollar meal when you don't exactly know where you could end up tomorrow.

Mid conversation with the workers on plan and pay, I caught a glimpse of Zeke who was navigating the crowd with the same smile on his face and carrier case in tow. He had been through this type of routine before, and he looked at ease as he navigated the crowd.

We, on the other hand, were awkwardly scrambling as I looked at a map for directions. I was trying to find the route to Murk Alley, a somewhat precarious area that was walking distance from the station. I had booked us a room at The Boisterous Boar Inn, which was all I could find within our means that had a rentable storage room large enough for Alex's apparatus nearby. I can be honest. It was not as if I wouldn't make the trek through the alley by myself if I had to, but when I first saw Murk Alley my immediate thought was how thankful I was to have someone with me. "Safety in numbers," I thought. However, that thought flew out the window as soon as Alex opened his mouth.

"Are you kidding me, Janie? I thought you had researched this place!" His eyes were darting around in his head.

"Well, it's within our budget," I huffed.

"We're going to get mugged or worse. Don't you watch movies?" He half whispered, half mumbled under his breath so the workers wouldn't hear. "This is the part where a guy in a mask steps out and blocks the path before cranking a chainsaw."

We picked up the pace a little. I saw the sign for The Boisterous Boar ahead. Outside the front of the establishment, we thanked the gentlemen for obliging us. I was glad we paid them up front because handling money in the open there could have made for unwanted attention.

Opening the door, a small bell clanged and we scanned the entryway ominously. A little old lady sat behind a shabby desk under a dirty overhead lamp fixture. She was nonchalantly reading a harlequin romance novel and jerked her head up when I cleared my throat.

"You checking in?" She was gruff at first but eased after inspecting our precautious faces.

"Yes, ma'am. It should be listed under Janie Morgan," I waited for her response.

"Okay. I've got you down for two beds, one bath; that'll be room two hundred and three."

We settled up and she handed me a key.

"Mind your step on the stairs; we're making some repairs," the lady looked over the top of her glasses and half smiled. "Enjoy your stay."

We trudged up the stairs and around a gaping hole in the right side of the third step from the top. I could just hear the million exaggerated reasons of how it got there running through Alex's head.

I fiddled with the key until it fell into the groove of the lock and turned the door knob. The room was pretty drab and had a musty mothball smell to it. There was one window in the center of the farthest wall, through which the sunlight came in and bounced off of dust particles. Two humble looking twin beds draped with faded navy quilts sat on each side of the room. I threw my suitcases on one and sat on the edge.

"I guess concierge and room service are out," Alex said with a raised eyebrow.

"It could be worse. There could be bugs." As I finished the sentence I walked in the bathroom to find two roaches perched on the side of the tub twitching their antennas. "Scratch that. We have some company already."

Alex peered in and frowned. "We have got to get some money up," he said as his throat constricted.

"All the more reason you should audition, huh?" I smirked. "Come on. I looked up the address to the cafe, and it's in the nice part of town. If we head out now, we'll have time to scout the area and get a feel for our surroundings before we meet Zeke."

I always preferred walking in a new place. It gives you more time to look around, and of course walking is free. We had about an hour until our rendezvous, so we started down the stairs, hopping over the broken step, and briskly walked out of the Boisterous Boar and towards the end of Murk Alley.

It seemed brighter and more cheery immediately once outside the alley. The streets of Aspirlington were filled with energy and had an air of opportunity. It had the same conglomerate of odd, pleasant, and pungent smells that many cities have. People were smiling and chatting as they passed us by on our walk along the sidewalk.

We continued along and discovered a small park with a fountain in the middle. Vagrant folk sat there with their head in their hands or holding cardboard signs. My heart always ached for them. Plus, seeing them made me feel ashamed. Whenever my path crossed theirs, I knew I had nothing to complain about, that I had no real problems. With the confusion that comes from having divorced parents, there were so many times I had felt like I didn't know where my true home was. But nevertheless, I always had a roof over my head, food on the table, and hugs from my family.

Among the people on the park benches, a sandy haired boy was taking two metal figure-eight looking hoops out of his bag. He pushed his bag underneath one of the benches and walked over to the front of the fountain. As he slowly lifted the figure-eights, he turned one clockwise with his right hand and turned the other counter clockwise with his left. It created a mesmerizing optical illusion. Shifting his feet alternately to each side, he began a routine of fluid circular patterns with the infinity shapes, building and creating even more captivating effects with each movement. Alex and I turned into the park to watch. The boy was tall and lanky but donned baggy, tattered clothing that swallowed him up. He couldn't have been older than twenty and had a kind yet solemn looking face throughout the routine.

After five minutes of being nearly hypnotized by the turning circles, I realized we had better get going. As we walked back toward the street, I wished I had money to spare for the street performer.

Another two blocks down we would find Braxton's Black Brew, and as we neared our destination, I felt oddly eager to talk to Zeke. Watching the sandy haired boy inspired me, and I needed to find the means to a better place of residence than the Boisterous Boar. This could be the first steps on the road to progress.

"I think this is it," I said to Alex.

The cafe was small but very quaint. The exterior of the building was painted a deep shade of burnt orange and had a small patio encased by waist high curling iron fence. From the roof hung baskets of dark purple flowers which led the eye up to a black sign stating Braxton's Black Brew in golden painted old English text.

I pulled open the door and was hit with the warm smell of vanilla and hazelnut. Tuning out the loud crunching of a coffee grinder, I scanned the room until I saw the small wave of a hand in the front corner by the windows. Zeke sat in a booth with a steaming mug in front of him.

"Hey! Thank you so much for meeting up with us," I said as everyone exchanged smiles and handshakes.

"No problem. I come here almost every day when I'm in town," Zeke replied. His smile was warm and sincere. He had a way of making me feel comfortable, even though I barely knew anything about him. "So what do you guys think of Aspirlington?"

"It's nice in the city, but we're staying at a place in Murk Alley that's not exactly luxurious."

"Murk Alley," Zeke's chin dropped. "Yeah, that's not a highlight of the city. You guys should watch yourselves around there."

"Duly noted. So, tell us about The Mandevilles' Marvelous Marvels," I nodded and changed the subject to avoid further humiliation.

"Right!" Zeke took a breath and set his folded arms on the table leaning closer, "Well, it was created by Reginald and Caroline Mandeville who have a history of circus experience since they were teenagers. Reginald performed with Carlyle's Carnival Of Wonders as an apprentice under the ringmaster, Carlyle, himself. Carlyle was also a sword swallower. He met Caroline in Artelandia while spying on a competing circus, Zingo's Symposium Of The Strange, for Carlyle. She was their lead contortionist. The story is that after watching her act, he waited for her outside her dressing tent for three hours. When she finally came out, he introduced himself and asked her if she would like to go stargazing with him that night. They say he told her that he bet there was no way he could find a star prettier than her, but wanted to give it a try. Smooth huh? Apparently she agreed and by the next day they were plotting to take the best parts of their circuses and start their own.”

“That’s so romantic,” I said with a bit of a sigh.

“Caroline packed her things and hopped a train with Reginald the next day. They headed back to the Carnival Of Wonders, and they both performed with them for a year or so. They implemented some crowd drawing aspects from Zingo’s, assuaging Carlyle for the new contortionist added to his payroll. Reginald said he simply couldn’t continue without Caroline, his star,” Zeke took a break to sip his cappuccino.

“So when did they start The Marvelous Marvels?” Alex asked, unfazed by any aspect of romance. Zeke’s expression shifted to a face of poorly hidden skepticism.

“There was an accident. Carlyle was found in his lavish hotel room, asphyxiated at his dining table in front of a half eaten lobster. Investigators reported that he choked on his food.”

“You seem a little unconvinced,” Alex stated flatly.

“Well, shortly after his passing Reginald inherited the circus as he was apprentice to the ringmaster. He and Caroline took over and pretty quickly started cutting performers that weren’t exceptional. They made it their mission to find the most rare acts to add to the show and changed the name of the circus.”

Alex’s face changed to an expression of suspicion.

“After three months into the show’s evolution, Reginald proposed to Caroline inside the ring. He had clown become ordained so they could have a ceremony at the end of a show; all the more money on ticket sales I suppose." Zeke rolled his eyes. "They've been traveling with The Marvelous Marvels for seven or eight years now."

"What made you decide to audition?" I asked.

"Well, I don't put all my stock in the rumors regarding their integrity. I like to form my own opinions of people's character. Plus, they travel everywhere on the Earth; many places I've only dreamed of going. If I can get on with the show, it's free globe trotting," Zeke smiled warmly. "What about you guys?"

"I've been training in the aerial arts for two years now. So when you mentioned the coming auditions on the train, it seemed kismet. The money couldn't hurt either," I shrugged with a grin.

"What about you?" Zeke shifted to Alex.

Alex was less prepared to answer. "Well, I play drums and I've been working on something that would heighten engagement of the audience during my gigs. Janie wants me to audition so I can finally showcase my invention."

"What do you call it?" Zeke asked.

"Actually, I haven't really thought of a name for it yet. You could call it a sort of—drum rollercoaster."

"Sounds like something I need to see. Very intriguing," Zeke said over his coffee cup.

"What about you? What kind of act do you perform?" I asked.

Zeke paused for a minute, "I'm a ventriloquist but I don't use dolls."

"What do you use?" I was puzzled.

"Well, my act is unique in that I perform ventriloquy with a highly trained chimpanzee," Zeke slowed his words down as he had been accustomed to heightened responses.

"A chimpanzee. Really?"

"Yes, his name is Tombo."

"Never seen that before," Alex smiled.

"Like I said. Unique," Zeke grinned. "Tombo was rescued by an animal research center and shelter that I worked for at the time. He was underweight and in pitiful health. I was tasked in overseeing his care during rehabilitation. Naturally, I fell in love and just had to adopt him. Then I started training him in oral motor movements to simulate talking. We've been best friends ever since."

"So that's what you had in the carrier case? The one with the stars," I asked.

"Yep, I try to keep him concealed to prevent a ruckus. He's quite beloved by everyone he meets."

"I can imagine. I can't wait to meet him," I beamed.

"He plopped into my life at just the right time. I think I needed him more than he needed me. Don't know what I would do without him now," Zeke said, staring into his coffee mug. "My parents had pretty much disowned me after I came out to them. So I followed a wild hair and moved to Tanzabia to work for the animal research center. I was far from everything and everyone I had ever known. I was on an adventure but felt like I had no one to share it with. Then I met Tombo, and he showed me unconditional love. Caring for him gave me a purpose."

"I'm so sorry," I said with a pause. "I can't imagine what it must be like to go through that. It's not fair."

"I have found that fairness and justice can be things hard to come by when you're different." Zeke sighed and tried to pull himself back to his cheerful mode. "But oh, being different makes life all the more entertaining," he said, making a gesture of grandeur with his hand.

"We're happy to have met you, Zeke," Alex said.

"Maybe the friendship can continue if we all nail the auditions," I added, invoking all the positive vibes that I could muster.

"I hope so. Traveling is so much more pleasant with friends," Zeke replied.

Chapter 3

Rosenburg Factory

I woke up to achy stiffness in my back and right shoulder after a night of uneasy sleep at the Boisterous Boar Inn. By the groggy sounds of his morning stirrings, Alex didn't fare any better. I saw out the window, through squinted sleep cornered eyes, that the sun had just peaked above the horizon in a foggy haze.

"May as well go ahead and get up," I mumbled to myself, as Alex stretched and snorted on the other side of the room.

I trudged to the bathroom, dragging my feet. After my eyes adjusted to the harsh cheap fluorescent light, the mirror revealed something that looked like a cross between Medusa and a frowning English bulldog. I would not be going to audition with a reservoir of beauty sleep.

After a semi-agonizing lukewarm shower, I twisted my hair into a tight, sleek bun. Once I had applied some eyeliner and mascara, I squeezed into my leotard and a pair of black and white vertically striped leggings. While Alex showered and prepared, I spent some time near the window sifting through my thoughts with Whisper.

I remember when I first met them. It was in a field behind my mother's house when I was about fourteen. I was having a rough day, filled with emotions about being stretched in every direction, trying to meet everyone's expectations. I wanted to go home, but I didn't know which way to go. Tears welled up and sat on the rims of my eyelids. Slowly I felt a warm sensation through my arms and torso, like a soft hug telling me I wasn't alone. My heart felt like it was being pulled out of my chest. As I stared at the tall grass blowing in waves across the field, I heard a quiet comforting voice ask, "Would you trust me to heal your heart?"

If anyone were an observing bystander they would've heard nothing but the breeze softly rattling the grass and see nothing but a girl struck with wonder and hope. Whisper speaks to you as only they can. It is beyond human understanding, but undoubtedly true and authentic.

I answered Whisper's questions with a shaky yes, unsure of what allowing them a position in my life would look like. Ever since that day it has been a journey of getting to know them, learning to trust them, and evolving a friendship unlike any earthly one. Lots of others before me had met Whisper, and many more would, but each relationship is different and treasured.

Whisper had been present at every destination of my travels. They were my constant. Talking to them made me feel at ease and hopeful about the coming events of the day.

Alex emerged from the bathroom and I snapped out of my quiet reflection.

"You ready?" he asked.

"Of course I am," I said calmly with a steady smile.

"Good, because we're gonna have a time getting my drum set there. I'm gonna have to pay some guys to help transport part of it, but I could use a hand for the blueprints and the cymbals."

"You got it," I saluted.

On our walk to auditions we passed the park where the sandy haired boy had performed. I glanced around looking for him, but he was not there. Four blocks further and six blocks east, we came to a very large and very dated warehouse. It was built of crimson colored brick and had two floors, each lined with double stacked twelve pane windows. We stepped up into the entryway and saw an iron plaque that read Rosenburg Factory 1889. Underneath the plaque was an easel sign that said *Auditions for Marvelous Marvels will be held in Suite 2007.*

Our hired help huffed and puffed as we shuffled through the hallways looking for the right room. We stopped them at suite two thousand and let them deposit the large bass drum and toms at the edge of the hall. Alex sat down his load as I shrugged my backpack off my shoulders.

I could hear music and ruckus down the hallway, seeping out from the auditions. A loud destructive commotion followed. While Alex rummaged through his backpack, I eased down the hall and peeked through a partially opened door. I could see a short Asian man running around frantically amongst a pile of broken chairs up on a stage. At the front of the stage was a long table where three people sat. A woman with long light blonde hair on the far left, a burly square shouldered man with dark hair in the middle, and a skinny young man on the right.

"While your dismount was near perfect, a chair balancing act would be much more impressive if it didn't have such a splintering ending," said a robust and chuckling voice from the man in the middle.

I was watching intently and starting to feel sympathetic for the performer.

"What are you doing?" came a fast, urgent voice behind me.

I twisted around so quickly I stumbled backwards on one heel and nearly fell down. My eyes found the direction of the voice and I saw Zeke muffling laughter.

"Sorry, I didn't mean to scare you that badly," he said, pulling the corners of his mouth down to convey his feeling.

"I guess I'm already nervous," my eyes darted back to the crack in the door, "though apparently not as much as that poor guy."

Zeke glanced inside and clicked his tongue, "Yeah, I'm afraid that may be a no go."

"NEXT!" came the loud yet cracking voice of the skinny man after he was elbowed in the arm.

A familiar face walked across the stage carrying a metal figure eight in each hand.

"Hey! I recognize that guy. We watched him at the park," I whispered.

"Oh yeah," Zeke too was watching keenly, "I've seen him perform there too. He looks pretty young, but he's super talented."

"What exactly is it that he performs?" I turned to Zeke.

"It's called poi," he replied. "It's a type of dance that originated in New Zealand, I believe."

The sandy haired boy began his routine turning the metal figure eights, starting with only the right hand at first, and then adding the left hand, and alternating directions fluidly. He shifted his feet and moved like a walking robot toward the direction of the blonde woman, who let her head drop to one side when he stopped in front of her. She gently nudged the arm of the man in the middle with the side of her right fist. He turned his pronounced chin towards her, but didn't budge otherwise.

The sandy haired boy shuffled and shifted his feet to the other side of the stage in front of the skinny young man on the far right; who was scribbling something down on a pad of paper in front of him. He pushed it towards the man in the middle.

The poi dance continued its flow until it reached center stage.

"You may stop, dear boy," the man in the middle spoke assertively. "Where do you perform this act typically?"

"Overlook Park, sir," the boy replied.

"For the public then?" continued the man in the middle.

"Yes, sir."

"And how do they respond to you?"

"Well sir, some people stop and watch," the boy answered anxiously.

"For how long?" The man was drilling him with a fixed gaze and flat affect.

"Some people watch for ten minutes, others more, others less."

"Less than ten minutes, you say?" the man's tone was turning cynical.

"Some people are in a hurry I guess," said the sandy haired boy turning his gaze to his feet.

"If I was performing in public, people would forget what they're in a hurry over. I make sure my performances get their attention and keep it."

"Yes sir, I'm sure," the boy replied, still looking down.

The blonde haired woman spoke up in a buttery smooth voice, "It's very captivating, your act. I'm just not certain it's quite energetic enough."

"Thank you, ma'am," said the boy quietly.

The three of them mumbled critiques for a minute.

The skinny man on the right abruptly said, "Thank you for your audition. You may go now."

The sandy haired boy nodded quietly and walked off the stage, along the side of the room, and towards us at the door. We jumped back and pretended to be unnoticing, shuffling around with our props and equipment. The boy glanced around the hallway dodging eye contact, though Zeke attempted to shoot him an encouraging smile.

"I hate that. He seems like a hard worker," Zeke murmured quietly.

"Yeah, and they seem a little harsh," I replied. "I don't know if I can do this."

"Sure you can. Think of it this way, if it's meant to be, it'll happen." Zeke's voice had a bit of a calming effect, even if only momentarily. "I guess I better go get Tombo."

He patted me on the back and walked down the hallway and into a nearby suite. I walked over to Alex, who was propped against the wall looking through his sketches of the drum coaster track. He appeared totally at ease, in his own little world. I realized he wasn't nervous at all.

"You're totally chill about this, huh?" I asked.

"Hey, I know my idea is awesome. If they don't like it for their show, they can watch me perform as a superstar when I'm rich and famous." Alex was half sarcastic, half serious.

"Who here is auditioning?" The skinny man had stepped out into the hallway. He stared at the two of us with his eyes bugging out. "Well?"

I pushed Alex's shoulder forward, and he jerked around to scowl at me.

"You?" the skinny man asked, looking at Alex.

"Yeah, I'll have to set up though," Alex answered with a snap of edge. He wasn't one for ill-mannered talk or impoliteness.

"You get five minutes," the skinny man spun around on his heel and walked back in the room.

Alex rolled his eyes. "You think we're gonna be able to work with these people?"

"We waited tables in a tourist town. This should be cake," I replied. "I'll help you bring some drums in."

Alex and I apprehensively started dragging equipment into suite two thousand seven. It was nothing for him to haul the large bass drum up the stairs of the stage, but I was awkwardly trailing and hit the railing with a cymbal. The clang made the blonde haired lady jump.

"What do we have here?" said the man in the middle.

"You have a musical act unlike any you've ever seen before," Alex huffed like a smart aleck.

"Oh really?"

"Yup, your buddy over there gave me five whole minutes to set up so I'll show you then," Alex said with a backhanded chuckle.

"What's your name, son?"

"Alex Burton, sir."

"Alex, it's nice to see someone with a little moxie in here. I am Reginald Mandeville, ringmaster of this spectacle."

"Thank you for the opportunity, sir," Alex replied, more at ease.

"And who is your noisy help there?"

"This is Janie Morgan. She will be auditioning as well," Alex threw a teasing look at me. No doubt he was becoming more irritable that I had dragged him into all of this. I made a slight bow for the sake of forgiveness. When I stood up, it was the first time I had a facing view of the man in the middle.

Reginald was quite handsome. He had high cheek bones and a very square chin. His umber colored hair framed his face with subtle waves and his brown eyes were striking. However, there was something in his half smile, or grin, that made you feel the need to proceed with caution.

"And what will you be performing, Janie?"

"Aerial silks, sir," I replied.

"Well, we already have an aerialist," Reginald snapped his fingers towards the skinny man. "Go get Shay, would you Anthony?"

I didn't respond. I felt that I had already failed the auditioned before I even introduced myself.

As Alex was completing the last bits of setting up, Anthony returned from backstage with a tall and slender, honey almond skin toned woman. Her beauty was flawless and intimidating, but upon introduction her smile warmed the room.

"Hi, I'm Shay," she greeted me. Her voice was pleasantly raspy.

I stuck out my hand, "I'm Janie, nice to meet you." Her grasp was dainty, but her hand had callouses similar to my own.

"Anthony tells me you perform aerial arts."

"Yes, I've been at it for a few years now," I replied.

She smiled genuinely, "I've got some silks already rigged if you'd like to use mine for your audition."

"Oh, that would be so great. I'm afraid I've already made a poor impression while helping my friend set up on stage."

"Nonsense. Reg is definitely tough, but just try to stay focused. I'll be looking forward to seeing your audition."

The pressure intensified. Another set of appraising eyes would critique my performance.

"Alright, Mr. Burton. Let's see what you've got for us," Reginald's voice abruptly cut through the room.

Alex stood behind his set. He executed a perfect back flip that landed in a handstand. From the handstand, he repositioned to bear his weight on his forearms directly in front of the bass pedal. One handedly he counted off with the bass drum in a simple beat, pressing the pedal with one hand from his inverted balancing act. Then he quickly reversed all the previous movements until he flipped and landed in front of the set again.

He dropped on his throne and snatched up his sticks, spinning them in front of his chest and over his head like a ninja. He began with a rapid soft trill on a high tom. Stretching his right arm behind his head to the left side of the drum set, he hit soft cymbal tings; tap a few beats, ting, tap a few beats, ting. His arms looked like they were revolving around his head.

Alex was picking up speed but making us all wait for the full intensity. He proceeded to perform a one handed string of beats coupled with double bass pedaling. His other hand held a drum stick and extended straight ahead, as if he was signaling to lead a charge onward. The Mandevilles' eyes were growing wider. Alex then tore out into a raucous slamming of all the drumheads, arms flying up and down, crossing and uncrossing in front of him. The volume was increasing. He spun both sticks in between each strike as he went.

Like the conductor of his very own orchestra, he slowed again. His left hand now extending to hit a glockenspiel. The mixture of its tones amongst the drum beats made it sound like two people were playing. As mouths in the room dropped, he slowed but continued the airy resonation. And after a few more beats of this, he slowed to a complete halt. Everyone's eyes were on him. Alex let out a loud resounding scream and lit into a full assault on the drum heads, cymbals shattering at full intensity. He began to pick up speed. I could see the muscles in his thighs tensing as he pedaled the bass drum. The veins in his arms were bulging, and sweat droplets flew off the tips of his hair as he slung his head. The faces he made looked like he was performing a Hawaiian Haka.

With the high hat clashing, and cymbal ringing, Alex maintained the beat. But as he did so, he intermittently leaped up, pulling his knees to his chest in between strikes. After a few of those he jumped high enough to stand on the drum throne, slamming like mad on the toms as he went, and upon returning to sitting he initiated the finale.

His whole body was moving so fast it looked humanly impossible. Each limb was moving separately from the rest of every other part of his body. The veins in his neck were now visible and his face was turning red. The sounds of the drums were like an explosion of fireworks. The final beats spaced out like the last three pops of a black cat fire cracker.

Alex always wore my ears out by going on and on about the importance of utilizing dynamics if you want to keep the audience's attention. This time he had outdone himself.

Alex's arms flew down, his chest was heaving. I watched mouth agape and noticed that I had begun to sweat too. Seeing him like this had an effect on me, though I'd never admit that to him. My pulse was up and I tried to swallow, but my tongue felt dry. He glanced toward me and I had to quickly shake it off. I signaled finger guns and a thumbs up awkwardly.

"Excellent showmanship," Reg said. "Really, very impressive. But what do you think makes this circus worthy?"

"This does," Alex tossed a scroll of paper at Reginald who caught it in one hand.

He rolled it out and across the table. The blueprint of the drum coaster. Reginald's eyebrows raised.

"This section will follow the track up and over inclines and declines. It'll travel across the whole room, over people's heads. He pointed. When it gets here, it will lock into a new track, a vertical ring. That ring will send me entirely upside down," Alex's breathing was slowing back to normal.

Reginald scanned over the prints, eyes darting, and then rested the paper on the table in front of him as he sat deep in thought. "Let me guess. The track is yet to be financed."

"Correct. The platform is complete, but the track is not. You could be the first to exhibit it. It's perfectly designed in the blue print. You'd just have to supply and assemble."

"You're asking an awful lot when you are the one who's auditioning to work for me," Reginald emphasized his statement with direct and unwavering eye contact as he spoke.

"Think of it as an investment," Alex responded as if he couldn't care less. And truth be told, he probably couldn't. If this didn't work out, he would find another way.

Reginald eyed his confidence and posture meticulously for a moment and then responded, "I like it, boy. You're in."

Alex looked to me with vague semi surprise and an air of smugness.

"Miss Janie, was it?" Reginald sarcastically implored, "Your friend's will be a hard act to follow, but I believe now is as good a time as any for your debut. Won't you show us your utmost pizzazz?"

"Yes, sir," I replied quickly.

Reginald was looking down his nose at the papers and notes on the table before him and curtly responded, "K."

Alex gave me an encouraging nod, and I walked up the steps to the platform. Shay emerged from side stage.

"These are the usual nylon tricot," she said as she lower the silks from the rigging to untie the daisy chain. "No fear of falling, only the thrill of flying," she said with a heartened wink as she adjusted and secured the rigging.

The silks were a rich, deep red that would pleasantly contrast my black and white outfit. I looked up from beneath the rigging and shook the two long flowing pieces of fabric to straighten and separate them. Alex had set up to play a simple yet beautifully brooding piano score. I signal him to press play.

As the music began, I split the silks and began with a *crochet climb*, in which I would invert upside down and wrap one leg. Then I would swing the other leg toward the ground to shoot myself to a higher hold above me. It always reminded me of a marionette doll. When I reached the top of the rigging, I was still upside down like a bat hanging in its cave. I wrapped the silks to cross the small of my back and around in front of me. Then I attempted to roll as smoothly as possible, articulating each vertebrae in my spine, until I was back into an upright position. Secured in the air, I had a silk in each hand that I could flap like wings as I gracefully stepped through the air like a flying pegasus.

I inverted again to catch the silks with my knees, adjusted them to rest on my shoulder, and hung in a cradle. I gazed at the ceiling as if lost in thought while I relaxed in a hammock, moving my arms slowly in alternating directions with loose extended fingers like a ballerina. I adjusted the crossing of my legs, and with another invert I was back to my bat like position upside down. I pushed the silks straight forward while pulling one leg out to roll a silk over the knee. I had completed the harness. With bent knees, I used my abdominal muscles to swing my body back and forth like a trapeze artist. Once I had achieved enough momentum, I grabbed the silks above me and was upright again, perched as if on a swing set.

After wrapping the red silks around each leg like candy canes, I arched my back as much as I could bend it. The pose looked like a C shaped back bend in the air. From there, to flip three hundred and sixty degrees, all I had to do was let go with my hands. After a slow exhale, I released my hands and tumbled forward in an angel drop.

There was no applause. The room was still quiet except for the piano notes. I unraveled and descended down to the center of the stage as slowly and gracefully as I could muster.

Flipping through the air was nothing new, but my breathing had increase from the anxiety of having all the pairs of eyes in the room focused on me. Finally, I heard soft clapping from side stage and turned to see Shay smiling.

"Great control and pose," she was saying as Reginald cut her off.

"Well, I can't say much for your pizzazz. Kinda slow for my taste," he stated flatly.

The blonde haired lady interjected, "I don't know, I found it maintained a fair amount of entertainment in the gracefulness and fluidity of movements."

"You always take up for the women, Caroline."

Anthony remained quiet and scribbled a few notes down.

"I perform with other apparatuses too. They allow faster transitions and spinning," I responded somewhat eagerly.

"We already have an aerialist," said Reginald.

I felt the sinking in my chest and my chin started to fall until Shay spoke up.

"I think she has potential. With some of my conditioning and adjusting, we could make something out of her."

"And you're going to take responsibility for her then, is that it?" Reginald looked dubious.

"Sure, I can handle that. Besides, I need her if we're going to do any double aerialist routines," Shay granted, though she looked somewhat apprehensive.

"Shay, I believe in your capabilities, but if she falters… it's on you. And she'll be out despite what port we happen to be in," said Reginald.

Caroline gave an agreed nod of approval and there was an agonizing moment of silence. Her sharp eyes paired with a half smile, "Welcome to the circus."

I tried to remain calm as I scurried to tie a daisy chain in the silks and briskly walked off stage.

"I've had all I can stand for the day," Reginald huffed apathetically.

"There's one more audition left, sir," Anthony said. "Mr. Zeke, you're up."

Chapter 1

Tombo

Zeke walked into the room holding the hand of an adorable chimpanzee. After a quick smile at the judges, he looked down at his partner in a reassuring manner.

"Ladies and gentlemen, this is Tombo."

Tombo stood as tall as Zeke's hips, his long hairy arms swaying as they walked. He was dressed in a pair of red shorts with gold stars on them and royal blue suspenders.

"Oh my goodness," breathed Caroline as her eyes grew bigger and a smile spread across her face. "He is so charming."

"What's your act, young man?" asked Reginald.

"I'm going to be performing ventriloquy with my friend here," Zeke answered.

"Ventriloquy? With a live animal? I don't believe I've seen that before." He glanced to Anthony and raised a large bushy eyebrow. Anthony perked up a little. "Good luck to you then. Begin when you're ready," he said indifferently.

Tombo let go of Zeke's hand and hopped up on a stool so that he was almost eye level next to him.

"Good evening ladies and gentleman! I'm Zeke and this is my brother Tombo."

Tombo's face looked surprised, and he began to move his lips and speak. I glanced at Zeke and the very subtle trembling movement at his Adam's apple. He maintained a bright and beautiful smile, pearly whites shining in the stage lighting, and looked out at the imagined audience in his mind.

"Brother? I barely consider you a friend," Tombo looked incredulous. I was surprised to hear that Tombo had an English accent, but it suited him quite well.

"Scientist say we share a common ancestor."

"Then I guess what they say is true, unfortunately. You don't get to pick your family."

"Oh come on, Tombo. You've come around to enjoying our friendship a little, haven't you?"

"You're alright," Tombo said indifferently.

"Well, regardless you need me. I'm the one who gives you a voice!"

Tombo furrowed his brow at Zeke and swatted his hands down in a dismissing gesture.

"Let's see what it would be like if I took it away."

Tombo's lips flapped, but no sound was heard. I saw Caroline's smile grow.

"Oh, I don't like to fight with you, Tombo. Let's take this out on the judges instead."

With that Tombo and Zeke both kept their lips closed, yet each of their voices were speaking again. It was Zeke's demonstration of just how professional his ventriloquy was.

"Now they don't know who is doing the talking," came the sound of Zeke's voice, though his lips did not move.

"Yes, maybe I'm the real ventriloquist here," the sound of Tombo's voice was heard, although his face looked completely frozen.

"We could switch voices too!" Zeke lips moved again, but this time Tombo's English accent was heard.

"I don't want your voice. It's not a strong, burly, manly type of voice," Tombo's lips moved but he sounded like Zeke.

"Fine, back to normal then."

"You need to work on that. I prefer to be friends with brutes of strength and robust vigor," Tombo said, flexing his arms in a double bicep pose to the panel in front of him. Reginald gave him a hearty laugh of encouragement.

"Oh, do explain the traits I should exude to meet your petty standards of toxic masculinity," Zeke acted miffed.

"Adventurous type, athletic type. You know. A man's man. I need to jump, and swing, and climb."

"I'm a man's man," Zeke retorted, looking offended.

Tombo made the funniest expression and raised one of his eyebrows dubiously.

"That's a topic reserved for more familiar company," said Tombo.

"OH, Tombo!" Zeke exclaimed and rolled his eyes. "Alright, since you like the strong silent type, why don't you give the audience a little exposition on your brawn and daring agility."

Tombo winked at the audience and executed a backwards somersault, landing perfectly back in place on the stool. He turned to face Zeke and put his hands on his hips, pausing as if to say, "Watch this."

He cartwheeled atop the stool three times, making revolutions but not inching forward, so that he continued to maintain movements perfectly synced and landing in the middle of the stool. On the third cartwheel he paused in a hand stand, his hairy legs straddled out and then came together to clap his feet instead of his hands. Next he lifted one hand from the stool, like a star teetering on one point, and then gracefully returned to his upright stance. Then, in an extremely well rehearsed manner, he leaped atop Zeke's head and balanced momentarily before back flipping off of it and back to the stool.

Zeke feigned shock as he dusted off the top of his hat. The judges were actually laughing. It was the first I had seen of an authentic smile on Reginald's face, though it was hidden by his enormous mustache. I could see the sparkle in his eye of a young boy. Caroline's eyes were wide and Anthony was nodding toward Zeke.

"Show off," Zeke said.

Tombo held up a loose shaking wrist, "You're up."

Zeke stepped forward on the stage. He brought both arms loosely flexed in front of his chest and obtained a ballet first position; his feet together at the heels and toes facing opposite ends of the room.

That was when I noticed his black ballet shoes.

Zeke stepped, extended a leg, and began pumping a string of fouetté turns. He increased in speed and then bent the knee of the extended leg to pirouette even faster for a few rotations. Landing in a fourth position, he gracefully turned and leapt into a very high grand jeté, legs completely split in mid air. Landing smoothly, he circled the stool and stopped beside Tombo again; taking a curtsy in triumph.

Zeke smiled at Tombo and took a deep breath, very satisfied with himself.

Tombo looked into the imaginary audience and appeared to convey a look of retort that said, "See the difference?"

"Oh, Tombo. Don't you think it's fair to say I have strength and agility? Just like you ordered." Zeke gave Tombo a smug and playful look.

"I guess you could say that."

"Since I indulged you, I think it's only fair that you return the favor," Zeke winked coyly.

"Cheeky bugger," Tombo said as he shook his fuzzy black head rapidly side to side. "What do you want?"

"Tombo, I know you have a soft side. And I know you're quite the singer."

"I do love a nice harmony," Tombo scratched his head. "If I pick a song for us, you can't get all sentimental. I've got a reputation to uphold."

Tombo jumped down and pulled a single 45 record from his carrier case and placed it on the player at the back of the stage. As the intro began he ran and jumped back onto the stool next to Zeke, who was fanning himself as if he might cry at the sound of the coming song. They alternated singing lines in the verse of an old song about relying on the help of a friend to conquer heartache.

As they harmonized the chorus I heard the panel excitedly whisper, "How can he make two different voices simultaneously?" Their eyes were starry and jaws slightly heavier.

Zeke and Tombo's song continued with great feeling and ended with a crescendo of the last verse in the chorus. Tombo hugged Zeke, his head pressed against his chest under his chin, and then they parted and high-fived each other.

All three judges stood and applauded as Zeke bowed and Tombo nodded his head vigorously up and down, showing all his teeth in a great smile. He even clapped his hands together for himself.

"That was fantastic," said Caroline. "I'm sure your act is one of a kind."

"Yes, well done," Reginald shot a look at Anthony and followed, "We would like to have your act as part of our show."

Zeke was beaming and his face started turning pink.

"What do you say?"

"When do I start?" Zeke said, with a half excited half nervous laugh, "It would be an honor to be a part of the Marvelous Marvels." He regained composure, trying to remain professional, as Anthony continued to stare at him inquisitively.

Alex and I stood against the wall like a pair of high schoolers.

"Well, they did a one eighty in morale once they saw Tombo perform, didn't they?" I mumbled under my breath with a giggle.

"All right, Anthony, I'd say we did pretty well today," Reginald turned around to face those of us still remaining from the auditions. "Folks, welcome to the Marvelous Marvels. My ship will be ready to push off at seven o'clock tonight, so you best be on it if you want to ensure your position as part of this circus. I wait for no one. We leave out of port Terindo and you're expected to transport and secure all of your own cargo. That includes giant drum coasters." Reginald shot a snarky smile and wink at Alex. "Once you're there, Anthony will direct you to male and female quarters. Shay, you'll bunk with your new responsibility… I mean roommate," another flicker in his eye. "Animals are housed in the lower quarters."

Zeke raised a hand, "Mr. Mandeville, I really would like to have Tombo in my quarters."

"He'll be fine, my boy. Your quarters will be a short walk away."

Zeke looked very reluctant, but half nodded.

"I bid you all adieu." Reginald jerked his head toward Caroline, who stood on command, and then together they strode out the door.

"Somehow I already feel an urge to start a mutiny. I haven't even boarded the ship," I said to Alex.

"Looks like Ol' Reg is gonna be a 'my way or the highway' kind of guy."

Shay was at the top of a ladder, taking down the silks and rigging. Zeke gave Tombo a rub on the head and ushered him into his star spangled carrier case. Everyone was dispersing. The stage and room felt cold and hollow without the colors and sounds of the circus acts; I felt the walls of the room were sad to see it go. Rays peering through the dirty rusted windows illuminated the dust in the air as everything steadily quieted.

Shay walked towards us as we were gathering Alex's drums and handing pieces off to the men we had to pay double to transport all the way to port Terindo.

"Intimidation is the first line of action Reg uses to maintain control of his performers. Particularly the new ones," she grinned at Alex, "and the free-spoken ones. Janie, I'm looking forward to rooming with you."

"Yes, me too. Thank you, Shay."

Shay floated out with a grace that made her even more alluring. She seemed unfazed by all the rhetoric going on. Her shoulders still relaxed, her posture still poised. I wondered how one could remain so calm under all that discouraging talk. It had to be stressful under Reginald's authority. And nevertheless, she remained as serene as a ballerina. I hoped she knew how to handle him, as she seemed to imply, and could give me some pointers. I hoped she could turn my performance into something the Mandevilles were at least content with.

Anxiety was creeping in and my nerves began tingling. After being independent and on my own for so long, it was unsettling to feel like I would impose so much need on a total stranger. On someone who had seniority in my area of performance. Who highly influenced whether I stayed employed with the Marvelous Marvels. What if Reginald kicked me out once we were on the other side of the world?

"Ready?" Alex snapped me out of it. "At least this is the end of our stay at the Boisterous Boar."

"I can only imagine the living quarters Reginald has in store for us."

Chapter 5

Light Catcher

I wondered what kind of ship I was signing up to live on, but after years of wandering, I felt like I had seen it all. We made it just outside of port Terindo around six o'clock and I was surprised to see the amount of shipping containers lining the area. They were in all colors, some bright and some dull and rusted. We drew nearer and found that the mountains of stacks were so high it was difficult to navigate our way to the actual docking arena. I looked every direction, but the shipping containers were like a labyrinth.

"Couldn't they have posted a sign," I huffed.

"They did. Look," Alex pointed ahead.

"What? I just looked that way. There was no sign."

"Maybe you're losing it. I've suspected that for months now."

I swatted Alex's arm with the back of my hand, but there it was. A simple sign, a pointing hand that read *Marvelous Marvels*. It directed us to the right and around the corner of a taller stack of six or seven containers. How did I miss it? I scanned along the row in the direction of the pointing hand, and at its end were pink and green lights glowing over the top of the giant metal boxes.

After making our way around, we gathered the first distant glance of our new home.

It was a giant ocean liner, and from the view of its stern, I could see at least eight decks reaching up toward the night sky. All sorts of people were hustling and bustling along them carrying suitcases, hula hoops, bowling pins, and costumes neatly hung on coat hangers and zipped in clear plastic. Animals were being rolled through in cages. A rainbow of lights in blue, pink, green, and yellow were emanating amongst the various decks.

There was a huge screen projection on the stern. To the right was Reginald's face all aglow, a large smile topped with his bushy mustache, arms in the air, and holding his top hat in his right hand. To the left, Caroline in a sparkling sequin dress with puffy pink feathers on top of the large swirling curls of her hair. Her chin held high. Above their images read *Marvelous Marvels* in the historical circus font.

Higher still, above the top deck, the sky was clear and the stars were visible, scattered across the night in great quantity. The water below was reflecting the ship's rainbow of light. Sweeping the bottom of the hull was the ship's name, *Light Catcher.*

To the left of the ship was a wide gangway bridging vessel to land. I could see the silhouette of a small, round man with stubby limbs and a short neck leading a very grand elephant onto the ship. It seemed like quite the unusual match given the difference in size, but the elephant was slowly and graciously following the man's every move.

Alex and I walked down the row of containers, eyes wide and taking in all the enormity of what we had signed up to do. We approached, and I wondered how much distance I needed to keep from the great animal. The man leading him must have noticed our arrival because he began to repeatedly glance over his shoulder in our direction.

"Sh-sh-she's friendly," the short man said matter-of-factly, "h-her name is Eloise."

"She's beautiful," I replied.

"Y-you can come up. She won't hurt you."

Alex and I stepped up the gangway a little closer. The man turned to face Eloise, and I saw more of his appearance.

He had a big smile that showed all of his teeth as he reached high to pet the enormous elephant. His hair was trimmed neatly and parted to the side. You could see he took great pride in its styling. He had a flat nose and kind eyes that slanted upward. As he turned towards us, I could see all the traits at once and I knew he was born with Down syndrome.

"I-I'm Daniel," he said and stiffly shot his hand forward to greet us. While shaking hands he exuded a childlike excitement and openness.

"It is a pleasure to meet you, Daniel. And you too, Eloise," I looked up at the elephant's eye. It was framed with long lashes and peering at each of us. She laid the end of her trunk on Daniel's shoulder and he beamed.

"M-me and Eloise been friends long time."

"I can tell," said Alex warmly, smiling at their interaction.

"New?" Daniel pointed at us.

"Yes, we auditioned today."

"Roomies," Daniel pointed to Alex and gave a thumbs up as he nodded his head up and down.

"That's right, men's quarters," Alex replied.

"I-I gotta take Eloise home. See you guys la-later," Daniel smiled and turned around. He stroked the bottom of Eloise's ear and led her along the lower deck.

I watched them turn into a large entrance that must have been the menagerie. Other performers were in line, waiting to take their animals inside. Zeke was amongst them, his face looking heavy, and the carrier case in his hands. I waited to catch his glance and waved at him. He forced a smile and shrugged his shoulders in defeat.

"No talking Reg into it, I guess," Alex said glumly.

We walked up the gangway where another sign read 'new hires this way' with another pointing hand. People were milling about everywhere. Some obviously performers and some obviously ship staff, deck hands, or roustabouts. Our path split amongst two signs indicating men's quarters to the left and women's quarters to the right.

"Well, I guess we're on our own now," I said.

Alex slapped an arm around my shoulders and eyed my expression from the side, "Let's meet at the top deck at ten o'clock. Maybe, being adults, we won't have a curfew," Alex rolled his eyes and made a face.

I watched him trudge down the path to the left, looking side to side as he went. With a deep breath, I raised and dropped my shoulders heavily.

I proceeded in the sign's direction for women's quarters on the right, which led to a fairly lengthy hallway. The sconces that lit it were antiquated in a charming way. Gold colored paint and the type of bulbs that you could see the glowing coils within.

There were no names listed anywhere to indicate which room would be mine. Luckily, I spotted Shay opening a door to the right side of the hallway. I hoped that our room would have a window. I had spent my fair share of stays in small, dusty, moldy rooms, but always had a harder time fighting the feeling of being trapped if it had no window. And I was already starting to feel trapped just by the semantics of Reginald's faux warm welcome.

I knocked on the door and heard some shuffling behind it. It swung inward as Shay opened it, and I was relieved to see a small round window straight behind her. I could see the lights from the ship dancing on the still surface of the sea outside of it.

"Janie." Shay's smile was warm.

"Hi. I didn't see any names, I just happened to see you walk in. I'm rooming with you, right?"

"Oh yes, yes. Caroline has already moved Ava a few doors down."

I looked at Shay a bit puzzled.

"Ava was my roommate before, she's a hooper. You'll like her. She's a fireball, kinda like your friend."

"Oh yeah," I rolled my eyes. "Shay, I'm sorry I got you stuck with babysitting duty and your roommate kicked out. I'm already off to a rocky start."

"Nonsense, don't be so hard on yourself. Ava will be more than okay and I enjoy teaching, so everything is fine."

"I just don't want to mess things up, or Reginald to take it out on you."

"Listen, I'm not worried about Reg. Nor do I fear him."

Shay's face was smooth and solemn as she spoke. And I felt inclined to believe her.

"Can you teach me how to do that? Not worry about Reginald?"

"Once I get to know you, Janie, we shall see. But enough about Reg," Shay swatted her hands down to dismiss further inquiry of the Mandevilles. "Here is your bed and storage area. Make yourself at home."

As I glanced around the room, I saw that it was leagues above the Boisterous Boar's accommodations, even though it was pretty small. The walls were stained and varnished wood, a rich shade of brown that exuded cozy vibes. Two small beds, one on each side of the room, with plum colored comforters that actually had enough batting inside it to keep you warm. They didn't look all lumpy or worn, and they had been made up by the cleaning staff on board. There was a stow away shelf near the ceiling, and sconces with bulbs similar to those in the hallway above each bed. On the floor, which was wooden, there was an oriental rug of intricate detail and rich dark colors; navy and crimson, mustard and burnt orange, emerald green. Between the two beds and under the window was a small dresser with drawers. It was antique, with claw feet on its legs and a key hole in each drawer. But it was boldly painted a deep teal and had magenta colored knobs. On top of it sat a small vase of rather strange looking flowers.

Shay's side of the room was quite organized. Pinned to the walls were pictures of what must have been her family, and past circus posters featuring herself in extravagant costume. In her stow away I could see several books, though they had no title on the spine, a small globe, and a suitcase with a lock on it.

I began placing my things around my side of the quarters, and started to feel more at ease than I had been since we arrived in Aspirlington. The room was warm, pleasant, and smelt of Shay's perfume; a mixture of cinnamon and vanilla. I felt my shoulders slowly relax, and noticed my breathing had deepened.

"We have a heading, you know. Just heard it a while ago from Ava, who you'll discover seems to find out everything ahead of everyone else."

"Oh, yeah?"

"First stop is Merdwick."

"Can't say I've ever heard of it," I replied.

"It's an old sea town, repopulated due to the boom in the algae harvesting craze. People are buying it left and right. Claims to enhance your immune system, full of delicious antioxidants. Recently it was discovered that it could be used to make fuel. A couple of hot shot business tycoons started a company over there and people nearby suddenly had opportunities for employment. But what's interesting is its history before all that."

"I'm intrigued. Go on," I urged. I was discovering that Shay had a way with storytelling, like she had been doing it for years. Just enough information to keep you wondering and guessing. Not all that rattling on and on, as many women tend to do. Her face glowed as she spoke. I felt kind of like an excited kid about to hear the telling of an old ghost story by a bonfire.

"Well. The story is that way before it was the algae fuel pinnacle it is now, and the ghost town it was before that, it was a regular old sea port. Fisherman were in and out, making their living catching and selling great big tuna, Mahi, and shellfish. Divers frequented the area too. Researching the wide blue enigma that is the ocean. Then one day a fisherman sloshed up against the marina dock and frantically stumbled his way to the coast guard. He didn't even tie up his boat. He told officials that he had spotted a dead body floating on the sea surface. It appeared to be a woman, face down with long hair matted against her back. He said he felt as a citizen he needed to bring the body in to shore, return her to the family who must be looking for her. That way she would at least have a proper burial. The boat drew near and slowly drifted beside her as he leaned over the railing to get a better look. He claims that the body rolled over and hurled a spear directly at his head, missing by a fraction of an inch."

"What?—Come on. Are you hazing me, Shay?"

She shook her head.

"It landed in the boom behind him. He turned it in, trying to prove himself. It's still housed in a small museum there in Merdwick. I haven't even told you the craziest part."

I looked at her dubiously.

"He believes that when he stood again, after ducking to miss the spear, he saw the large slender body of a fish. Sage in color and tail wide as five feet. Diving back down to the deep."

"Mermaids?" I said disbelieving. "Shay, do you believe that story?"

"I don't know," she shrugged. "But after the coast guard saw the spear, they had it examined by a marine biologist. Then they sent divers to the area. And only one out of three made it back to the surface. The diver that survived was so shaken, she hasn't been in the ocean since. She said she saw a faint silhouette on the sea floor in the distance. The water was murky, and it was dark that day so visibility was poor, but she thought it looked like a sort of building under water. Next thing she knew, there was a red patch drifting up above the structure. Swimming a bit closer, she saw a snorkel mask floating back up to the surface."

"Maybe it was a shark that got them."

"Maybe it was, maybe it wasn't," Shay said, shrugging.

"Okay, well, why is that our first stop?"

"Like I said, it's repopulated now and this algae company is having a big end of the year social. They want ambience and entertainment. Most of the people who live in Merdwick work for them, so it's likely to be a large event. The whole town will probably be in attendance."

"A large crowd… I haven't really performed for more than a few people. So now I can worry about stage fright and mermaid spears."

"Performing in front of a big crowd is the same as performing in front of a small crowd. Just like performing five feet off the ground is the same as thirty feet in the air. It's your mind you have to control." Shay's calm tone was reassuring.

"When do we start conditioning and choreography?"

"Tomorrow morning."

"Where at?"

"There's a dining area right smack in the center of the boat. It's where everyone has their meals or hangs out during their downtime. And it just so happens to have the tallest ceiling. It's open all the way to the top deck because the architects that made the ship wanted a huge sunlight window above the dining area for sunsets and star gazing. There's a beam across the top landing for rigging and we have a roped off area below. So you may get used to audiences more quickly than you think."

I just stared at her blankly. "I can do this," I thought in my mind, initiating a inner pep talk. "This is a good thing. Get outside your comfort zone."

"You will be just fine. I'll be right there, too. You'll get to meet Ava," Shay listed her reassurances. "We're a team. Heck, we're a family. We look out for each other."

It was like Shay was reading my mind. I sighed aloud. "Well, I made it on board and I'm sure we'll be moving out soon. No turning back now."

"That's the spirit," she patted my shoulder.

"Oh, I told Alex I would meet him at ten o'clock. I promise to be quiet coming back in."

"Sure, I'll see you in the morning."

Chapter 6

Top Deck

I walked back down the hall, from the direction I came upon boarding *Light Catcher*. I had hoped to find a directory that would guide me to the dining area. It eased my nerves to see where I would perform before the actual time came. That way I could visualize myself being there. To get more mentally prepared and minimize fear of the unknown. Never mind the fact that this wasn't an actual performance, I'd only be practicing and conditioning. But it certainly felt more significant and consequential knowing that the entire crew, performers, and Mandevilles could be in and out at any given time; criticizing the new girl.

I felt it was very important to not only make a good impression, but to make good with as many people on the ship as I could. From the moment we set out to Port Terindo I kept thinking I would need all the support I could get. Because it sure seemed that the Mandevilles would drop the axe on me quickly and abruptly if I didn't prove my value in the very near future.

Signs led me from the outer viewing deck to the inner rooms of the ship which included a gym, sauna, reading room, snack counter, cocktail bar, various empty training rooms with the names of acts listed at the door, inside entry to the menagerie, and finally the dining area. And that was just the bottom deck of the enormous *Light Catcher.*

As I passed along the halls, I encountered a diverse variety of smells. Steam and sweat near the gym, pop corn from the snack counter, smoke wafting out of the bar as patrons walked in and out. This hall had the same amber lighting as the hall to our room. The carpet was emerald green with a golden crosshatch pattern. Nearing the end of the hall, I could see that it was opening to a larger space; the entryway to the dining room.

The room was very open and reached all the way up to a glass ceiling at the very top of the ship; through which I could see stars twinkling against the night sky. Green plants with towering sprigs of leaves, creeping vines, and tropical flowers were proudly manicured and arranged around the room near the tables and chairs which were white with gold legs. On the right side of the room was the queue area beside a glass topped buffet and a cash register, though dimly lit since it was closed.

At the back of the room, it looked as if the tables and plants parted to make an opening. I walked further in to investigate. Sure enough, I scanned my eyes up a long red silk that was rigged at the top beam under the great sun window.

"This is it," I thought in my head. Right now the room was dim and quiet, but I could picture the hustling and bustling to come. Shaking off the nerves, I looked to the left of the room and saw an elevator. It was beautifully geometrical and made of glass so that you could view the great room as you ascended or descended amongst the decks.

I went to it and pushed the button to go up. Stepping inside, I moved toward the glass to watch the ascent. It was then that I got a feel for just how high the silk were rigged, watching foot after foot of it pass as I rose in the air. It was much higher than any I'd ever used.

The sharp ding of the elevator bell broke my trance and I stepped off. Being hit with the warm smell of salt air and sea spray was a comfort. I had always treasured that scent and I was presently very grateful to smell it. I climbed another small set of stairs that led to the open night sky above the top deck.

I trailed my eyes across the deck, looking for Alex through the shifting green and pink colored lights I had seen from Port Terindo. They slowly waved across the night sky and I wondered what the sea life below must have made of it. Movement from the corner of my eye caught my attention and I headed to some wicker couches and chairs where Alex was lounging. I plopped down, flopping my arms onto my knees. Conversely, Alex looked at me bright eyed, like he had won the lottery.

"Isn't this great! To think we could be sitting in that dump of an inn right now wondering how we're gonna scrounge up for tomorrow's dinner," he said. "I don't know about you, but my room is nicer than the ones I've stayed in all year. And did you know meals are included for all Marvelous Marvels performers?"

He was talking so much and so excited, I could see it was going to be tough to get a word in.

"Turns out I'm rooming with Zeke and Daniel. Huh, what are the odds?" He laughed to himself, "They're gonna be fun. Daniel is hilarious!"

I interjected myself into the monologue. "Slow down, cowboy! Geez. I'm glad you're enjoying yourself." A yawn crept out, and I thought how funny it was that Alex was this jazzed up when I felt exhausted. I glanced up at the sky and felt comforted by its steadfastness. It remained the same, something one could rely on and expect to see at the end of each day.

"Okay, I know," he slowed. "Tell me about your room and Shay?"

"Shay is great. I couldn't have asked for a better roommate. She's been filling me in on the goings on around here. Looks like I'll be practicing with her in the dining area of all places. She says it'll build confidence."

"Nice, hah! Free entertainment for me and the boys."

"Alex, you know how I get, please don't make it worse."

"I'm kidding," he pronounced in staccato. "Chill out, we've got it made right now."

"This is just so easy for you, I know. Mr. Burton, drummer extraordinaire. Look at my coaster, watch me play upside down," I rattled in a mocking voice. "Some people don't get to just float along and enjoy the richy rich benefits nonchalantly."

"I'm not floating along," he interrupted sharply. "I've worked very hard at this and you know it. Not only that, but I've covered for us both when you've been running low." His face was hardening.

I knew my own stress had started this, but I couldn't stop myself from continuing, "I've never asked you to cover for me. I can take care of myself, thank you!"

"Well, I did anyway! I thought you and I were a team."

"We are!" I realized how high my voice had raised and tried to turn it down, "We are. And I'm grateful. I'm just nervous about how this is all gonna turn out."

"Okay. Don't take it out on me," Alex was trying to control his tone as well. "It's gonna be fine. I think Shay is going to have your back."

"It's easy for you and her. You both already have the Mandevilles' approval. You guys aren't going anywhere. Your spot is secured."

"You're just going to have to be strong and show them what you can do. You can. It's all up to you. Visualize it in your mind and go."

He drove me nuts with all his psycho babble and commentary, but I was so used to Alex being around. Looking out for me when no one else would. We'd been traveling together for a long time now. The thought of us getting separated, because I couldn't cut the mustard, was daunting.

"I know, I know," I sighed and decided to redirect the conversation. Maybe it would ease my anxiety to distract myself. "What do you think of your new digs and roommates?"

"I'm glad to be rooming with them. Zeke has been a little different though. Not quite as peppy," he made air quotes and wide eyes at the description, "since Tombo was put in the menagerie."

"I would be too. Tombo is amazing. I'd want him around all the time."

"Yeah, he is. Zeke said he tried to appeal to Reg, but it was no dice. Daniel has been trying to cheer him up, since Eloise is in the menagerie too."

"Tell me about Daniel," I said.

"He's so funny. Always happy, smiling, and he cares so much about others. I think he's the nicest guy I've ever met," Alex said, looking thoughtfully.

"I could see that," I replied. "Did you hear about our first stop?"

"Eh, Zeke mentioned some place. Mud duck or something."

"Merdwick," I rolled my eyes at him. "Shay told me some interesting stuff about it. She said it's rumored to be the home of spear throwing mermaids. According to legend that is," I said in a mocking tone.

"What the heck?" Alex made a face. "I guess I'll have to check if they have mer-shields available for purchase at the supply counter down stairs then," he said sarcastically.

"You could use your drum sticks to deflect blows. Like nunchucks."

Alex rolled his eyes.

I shrugged my shoulders, "I guess I should head back to the room. It's getting late and we start practice tomorrow morning. If you can humble yourself enough to watch supportively, then I guess you could come."

"I solemnly swear to try my hardest," he held up a hand like he was being sworn in a courtroom. "I'm going to see if I can have one of those training rooms to set up my drums in for practice. I'll wander that way when I'm done."

I stood up, stretched my arms toward the stars above us, and wished Alex goodnight. When I got back to my room, I quietly slipped underneath the warm covers of my new bed. I moved as gingerly as possible, so as not to disturb Shay's peaceful breathing and slumber. Again, I thought about how easy she makes this gig look. Staring at the ceiling, I laid restless, a million thoughts swirling around in my head that just wouldn't be quiet. I tried to shift my focus to Whisper and the fact that this circus was a means to an end, a stepping stone of the path to Fimaldi Hunu. Slowly the tension in my body eased and I began to drift.

I dreamt throughout the night. At first I was standing in a long thin dress on the top deck, staring across a flat glassy sea. Insidious circus music crept into my awareness, growing steadily louder. I spun around quickly scanning the top deck, but found no performers or any other people for that matter.

A strong gust of wind whipped my hair back, and I crossed my arms, trying to keep warm. Looking up, the sky became dark purple, and the clouds picked up their pace as if they were running away from something. I looked back at the sea and watched as it began to churn the water into waves so big that the *Light Catcher* itself began to sway.

I was staring at the ocean, trying to make sense of this rapid change in the mood of mother nature when a voice behind me said, "I think your time is up, deary. You just don't make the cut."

I turned back around to meet the cold dark eyes, like a great white shark, of Reginald Mandeville. His eyebrows rising and the edge of his lips curling with sick pleasure. He held up his cane and pushed my left shoulder back with it. He was pushing me to the edge. I turned around and saw there was now an opening in the ship's side, and a plank extending out over the angry waves. I turned back to beg him to stop, and when I did I saw the entire circus was in attendance, lights flashing over head in the angry sky like tonight was a celebration. Alex stood watching with a sad but solemn and defeated face. He wasn't making any move forward to help me.

Reginald was advancing, tapping me back with his cane so I had to step backwards. I was over the sea now, my heels at the edge of the rickety wooden board. "Send my regards to the merpeople," Reginald tipped his hat at me and then shoved the cane one hard last time, knocking me backwards and off the edge.

The sensation of fear and falling swam around my senses until my body couldn't take anymore and jolted me awake. The sound of thrashing covers and heavy breathing roused Shay up.

"Honey, are you okay? You've been talking in your sleep like crazy. Should've warned me about that, it's kinda scary," Shay's eyes were half shut.

"I'm sorry, Shay. Just a nightmare. Sorry."

"Alright then," she rolled over towards her wall in the cabin.

I did the same and fortunately drifted back to sleep pretty easily.

Again I dreamt. I was swaying back and forth amongst the giant waves, kicking and grasping at nothing with all my might. But slowly the sea calmed, and the sky brightened. The water began to feel smooth and warm, and I floated easily on top of the tranquil ocean. My hair rippling in all directions around my head, my face orange in the glow of a rising sun.

I knew this comfort came from Whisper. Then the dream faded, evaporating from sight, and I was back in darkness of dreamless slumber until the sound of my alarm woke me.

Chapter 7

Conditioning

I quickly dressed to catch up with Shay, who was already prepped for the first morning of conditioning and choreography. Together we walked to the dining area. As we passed other performers in the halls, they all greeted Shay with a morning salutation or a polite nod, though none of them seemed to take notice of me. Shay warmly replied to each greeting. By the time we had walked halfway there, she must have noticed that I was looking at the ground as I walked.

"You're new. You will get to know everyone in time," she reassured me, but she seemed to observe all these interactions with knowingness in her eyes.

The sun was beaming in from the skylight windows above and bouncing off of the greenery neighboring each table. People were shuffling around the room. Circus performers were getting their breakfast and socializing. The staff scurried around filling food trays with eggs and bacon, wiping off tables, and pushing in chairs that performers neglected. Their heads down and focused on their duties.

Shay and I sat together for a light breakfast at the tables near the silks rigging. I scanned the room for Alex or Zeke but saw no sign of them. Instead, I watched a blonde girl bounce her way to our table, a bright smile on her face.

"Good morning, ladies," she said. The sun beams lit up her sparkling blue eyes as she sat down at the table with us. "You must be Janie," she stuck out her hand to greet me, the first greeting I'd received all morning so far.

"Hi, yes, that's me," I replied.

"I'm Ava," she said, "Shay told me we were getting another aerialist. Welcome to the circus!" she bubbled, tossing her hand up in cheery animation.

"Thank you. Yeah, Shay told me I would meet you today. I know you guys were roommates. I'm sorry they put me in your spot."

"Oh, no. No worries. After three years with the Marvelous Marvels, I can just about room anywhere."

"Wow, that's a long time. How long have you been with them, Shay?" I asked.

"Five. Before that I was with Carlyle's Carnival of Wonders," she replied.

"She ended up here because Reginald poached her from them when he split," Ava said.

"That's true." Shay didn't elaborate and Ava switched subjects.

"So what's your act, Janie?"

"Well, I've been doing silks for a long time but I also really like lyra."

I had picked up lyra a year into silks training. It was a welcome change because it allowed for more free style flow, rather than wrapping silks to pose or execute a drop.

A lyra is a large metal hoop suspended by rigging, though it's usually closer to the ground than silks. A performer spins beneath it and can then invert to pose under, within, or above the hoop. I enjoyed how you could transition between tons of different moves and poses. When I was free-styling it felt more like a dance than silks. It was therapeutic.

"I didn't know you had experience with lyra," Shay perked up, "We could use another performer in the lyra routine. Would you be interested?"

"Of course. I'm here to serve," I laughed, "Maybe the Mandevilles will be more inclined to keep me around if I can do two apparatuses."

"Let's make sure we allow time for me to see you on the lyra today." Shay seemed genuinely interested. I smiled, feeling slightly more secured.

"Sounds good to me. What is your act, Ava?"

"I'm a hooper," she announced proudly, "that is hula hooping. I'm up to fifteen hoops now, and I also do balancing on a walking globe. You know, those four foot high balls of hard hollow plastic."

"That sounds cool. I can't wait to see," I said.

"She's amazing," Shay said as she smiled at Ava.

Ava waved a hand to stop her, "You haven't seen Shay perform yet, have you? She's the one that's amazing."

"Well, we better eat up because we need digestion time before we start swinging upside down," Shay said, "otherwise none of us will look amazing."

After we finished breakfast, Ava filled us in on the latest gossip around the circus, what she had heard about Merdwick, and about her recent break up with a juggler Reg cut from the show last month. She said that she just couldn't keep up the long distance relationship and that unfortunately he took it a bit harder than she did.

When Ava left, Shay made her way to the roped off practice area and began untying a daisy chain from the silks. The red fabric jumped as she pulled, shining in the beams of the morning sun. I sat down on the adjacent carpet to stretch, trying to inconspicuously tally the amount of people in the room. Most people had finished their breakfast, but were lingering around to socialize.

"Alright, let's start with some conditioning," Shay said.

She led me through grip strengthening work by tying a knot in the bottom of the silks to sit on. From my perch between the two silk, I held on and scooted backwards off the edge so that only my knees and hands held me. We held that position for two minutes as we alternated kicking our legs. My hands began to burn after the first minute had passed, but I dared not show it with my face.

I learned that to be a performer, you had to endure and hide pain. Like the ballerina breaking her toe nails, bleeding in hard wooden point slippers as she lands a grand jeté and pirouettes across a stage. Sometimes beauty is pain. Your face must remain smooth and smiling as if you felt nothing but euphoria.

In reality, silks sometimes cause friction burns, bruising in several places you wouldn't imagine, and muscle strains from over zealously hitting a back bend or split. Lyra's price was bruising like mad and monkey bar hands; callused, rough, and peeling. You can forget achieving a lady's delicate hand shake.

Consequently, many performers were good at hiding pain, physical pain and emotional pain alike. Although new to the game, I wasn't half bad at it myself.

Next we worked on core control by executing numerous sets of what was referred to as *tuck, pike, straddles*. This was performed by holding your body weight in between the silks, arms tightly flexed to your ribcage and feet pointed. Then pulling knees to chest, raising straight legs clinched together to a ninety degree angle, and then splitting legs as if to the west and east and raising to the same angle or higher. It was taxing to your abdominals as well as your hands and forearms.

We finished with climbing the silks to the top of the rigging and back down ten times; to a height I did not frequent. From the top, I scanned the dining area. Alex and Daniel were walking through the entryway and headed to a table in the middle of the room after grabbing some left over fruit. No doubt for optimal viewing of our practice.

Shay ran through her current routine, explaining each transition and pose, and then monitored my imitation.

"Okay, arch your back a bit more," she would say, "keep those legs straight and point your toes!"

Shay was helpful and gave instruction in an encouraging way. She celebrated my follow through. Despite the apprehension of knowing I was probably being watched by performers who had been around way longer than I, I felt more calm and grateful for Shay's positive energy.

I was starting to sweat and my breathing was audible when Shay said we could take a break. Her skin glistened like dew on the grass while I wiped beads of water off my forehead with the back of my hand. Ava rounded the corner, pony tail bouncing, a few hoops across her left shoulder, as I plopped down on the floor to stretch.

"You guys have been killing it, huh? It's a beautiful day up there, so I nabbed a practice spot under the sun," Ava beamed. She had changed into a sports bra and compression shorts, blue to match her eyes.

"A tan never hurts either," she said, winking.

Alex and Daniel must have noticed I was on break and walked over. I waved at them as they approached.

"Let me introduce you guys to my friend, Alex. You probably know Daniel, right?" I asked.

"Hi guys!" Ava smiled.

"Alex, this is Shay and Ava," I said as I pointed to each.

Alex extended his hand to Shay and then Ava, "Hi ladies." Daniel followed suit and shook each of their hands too. Even though they already knew each other the girls smiled and greeted Daniel just the same, giggling and patting his arm.

"How's Eloise doing, Daniel?" Shay asked.

"She good. I bet she's h-h-hungry now. She's always hungry," Daniel replied matter-of-factly and Alex muffled a laugh. I noticed Ava's eyes appraising his half grin.

"How long have you two been friends?" Shay pointed a finger to me and then Alex, no doubt remembering our awkward entrance into auditions.

"Too long," Alex smirked. "I can't get rid of her," he answered. I squinted my eyes at him.

"Sounds like an old married couple," Shay said.

"Definitely not," I stated flatly. Alex made a face like he was grossed out.

He turned his attention, "What do you do, Ava?"

Ava shrugged a shoulder to jostle the hoops, "Here's a hint."

"Only three?" Alex asked.

"Add twelve and a walking globe." Her smile somehow grew wider at his teasing.

"Okay—that sounds impressive," Alex flirted and then turned. "Shay, Janie says you've been a godsend of a roommate."

"I try. She's about to double down and show me her lyra skills," Shay winked at me.

"Good, make her work hard." Alex raised a bushy eyebrow and added, "She also mentioned that you encouraged her to be mindful of merfolk at our next port."

"Oh, she did, huh," Shay crossed her arms. "Well, it may be best for all of us to heed the warning that has circulated from the people of Merdwick."

"I-I've been to Merdwick. I-I saw one," Daniel interjected.

"One what?" Alex asked with a dubious expression.

"M-mermaid. Not nice though."

"Well, that's the story Zeke and I need to hear tonight then," Alex patted Daniel once on the back and then slung an arm around his shoulders. Daniel's grin showed all his teeth. "Ladies, it was nice to meet you."

We all watched Alex and Daniel head back out of the dining area. When I turned back to the girls, Shay looked at me but Ava continued to watch the boys, a smile still on her face.

"He's a pill, I know," I said.

"That is just so sweet how fast they've become friends," Ava swooned. "So many people ignore Daniel."

"Eh, maybe he's got a heart in there somewhere," I said, glancing back at Alex. "Alright, lyra?"

Shay set up the rigging and swivel and attached a hoop to the bottom of a spanset with a carabiner. She stepped back and gave the lyra a spin with the flick of her hand.

"Free flow. With music accompaniment. Don't worry, it's not *Entry of the Gladiators*," said Shay as she pressed a button on an old boom box. Soft piano seeped out of the tiny holes of the speakers. I soon recognized the classical melody. Shay extended her hand as if to say 'it's all yours.'

I peeked around the room before walking to the hoop. It was heightened so that the bottom of the lyra came just under a raised arm's length. From beneath, I wrapped my fingers around it and let my body sink just enough that I could initiate a spin with one leg. As the room began to revolve into a blur around me, I inverted and hooked a leg on the bottom of the hoop. A pose and then I pulled myself up into the center, with one leg bent along the hoop and the other straight toward the ground like the tip of a spinning top. I attempted my most flexible back bend and continued to spin. I loved this pose. It reminded me of the ballerina inside a jewelry box, like the one I had when I was a little girl.

From that point on, I forgot the people observing me. My world was turning and turning as the gentle prompts of ivory keys led me into a dance within a space above the ground, yet not in the heavens. The swirl of the motion so peaceful and calm. The melody guided me through a *birdie, flag, man in the moon,* and *shoulder mount* within the center of the metal circle. I inverted again from the top of the hoop into a *clock split,* and from there transitioned to a *hock's hang, skin the cat,* and *Russian split.*

I was feeling strong. Even despite all the work we had done conditioning on silks. I could hear Shay and Ava murmuring in between piano strokes, but felt confident it was positive. From the *hock's hang,* I fluidly slid around the edge of the lyra into a *lion in a tree.* Since I was positioned to look upward, it was then that I noticed a familiar face on the fourth deck. Caroline Mandeville stood near the edge, her forearms softly propped on the railing. In a slow and thoughtful motion, she brought an opera length cigarette holder to her red lips. My rotation had slowed and I could see that she was watching me from above.

I tried to maintain composure as I rolled through to a single knee hang from the bottom bar and descended back to the floor as slowly as I could control with my core. I looked to Shay, who wore an excited expression, and then up to the fourth deck. Caroline nodded with a small polite smile, acknowledging my attention to her presence, and slowly turned to step away from the railing. One hand dragging elegantly across the rail as the other lifted the cigarette to her pursed lips for another drag. Then she was out of sight.

"La lyra est ton don!" said Shay enthusiastically.

"Uh, what?"

"Lyra is your gift," she translated.

"Thanks. Do you think Caroline will approve?"

"I don't see why she wouldn't," Shay stepped closer and lowered her voice. "And on the subject of Caroline Mandeville, you need to be mindful and make as best an impression as you can if you spot her around. She is Reginald's eyes and ears around the troupe. She's probably on her way to report your new found talent to him right now."

"Carefully noted."

"She's the reason my last beau was fired," said Ava in whispers. "She had been watching the jugglers' practices, inconspicuously, for a few days after he shattered a glass bottle during our last show. Told Reg he didn't seem to have enough drive or diligence to be sure it wouldn't happen again. That he spent too much time at the cocktail bar and that he was overly distracted by me, by our relationship. Can you believe that?"

I spent the rest of the afternoon following Shay and Ava around the great *Light Catcher*, like a little kid sister. They gave me a full tour, introducing me to other performers along the way, though most of them did not seem too eager to waste their time getting to know a new act that wasn't sure to last. The trapeze duo was cordial, but their eyes seemed pained at the sight of me.

The lion tamer took one look at me and flat out said, "The Mandevilles will eat her alive, maybe more viciously than my lions would. Good luck, sweetie."

Master Kai, the strong man, didn't even speak a word to me, only nodded. But to be fair, he didn't speak much in general. There was only one veteran performer other than Shay and Ava that did not seem to judge me and always greeted me with exuberant kindness. And that was Daniel.

Shay led the way to the menagerie. Roustabouts scurried around carrying pails of fresh water, leading animals, carrying cages, and shoveling out the stalls. I watched them struggle and huff. Viewing the juxtaposition of occupations, I couldn't help feeling that I was not someone who belonged in the midst of Shay and Ava. Like I was an imposter.

The noise of tropical birds cawing, horses stomping, and the screech of a macaque monkey filled the large room which was spacious but still crowded by the animals.

"H-hey you guys!" I heard the familiar stutter and found Daniel near the largest stall.

"Hi, Daniel. How's big beautiful Eloise doing today?"

"She's okay. Sh-she doesn't like riding the ship as much."

"How does she like to travel?" I asked.

Shay interjected, "There are many other ways this circus may travel. You'll find out soon enough. We don't want to scare her away yet. Do we, Daniel?"

"No, no. It's okay, Janie," said Daniel. He hugged me with his stubby arms. I hadn't felt truly hugged in a long time.

"Daniel, are you giving my hugs away?" A playful voice came from the entryway. Fittingly dressed in a white t-shirt and black suspenders, boiler hat nestled on top of light reddish blonde hair, Zeke warmed the room with just the sound of his voice.

Daniel smiled as Zeke wrapped an arm around him, "I hope you guys aren't bothering my roommate."

"Ladies, this is Zeke. We met on the train to Aspirlington. He's the one who told me about the auditions."

"Very nice to meet you. You're an animal trainer, right?" Ava asked.

"Well, sort of. I'm a ventriloquist who uses a trained animal. Though it doesn't feel right calling Tombo a trained animal. He's more accurately described as my gracious little friend."

"Can we meet him?" Ava bubbled.

"This way," said Zeke. We all followed him to the corner of the menagerie. "It's killing me that he has to stay in here," he whispered as he held Tombo's hand from between the bars of his cage.

"He's adorable. Hi, Tombo," said Ava, smiling at the little chimpanzee behind bars.

"I don't know all the info, but I just heard that the circus travels in different ways," I said, playfully cutting my eyes at Shay. "Maybe next stop will be different."

"I think Reg is demonstrating his control. And unfortunately, you and Tombo may be the guinea pigs for the new hires to learn from. To drive home the idea that even the best performers are under Reg's orders," Shay said. "However, if you impress him enough in the first show, and the audience favors you, he may bend a little."

"Well, no pressure then," Zeke said sarcastically.

"Zeke, do you know where Alex is?" I asked.

"Last I saw him, he was headed to one of those private rooms for practice."

"Okay. Guys, I'll catch up with you this evening," I said to the four.

"See ya."

I headed to the practice rooms feeling hopeful about the kindness those four had shown me. As I walked, I started day dreaming we were all like a little family. But as soon as that pleasant thought entered my mind, I felt I had to shove it out. Sometimes getting your hopes up leads to more pain, and I didn't want to give myself the opportunity to be disappointed. I resolved to play it slow. I hadn't even made it through the first show yet.

As I walked down the hall, I peeped through small slender windows in the sound proofed doors of the practice rooms. In one window, a belly dancer with a snake draped around her shoulders. In another, a sword swallower who styled his hair and beard similarly to Reginald's. Eventually I found what looked like a madman beating the devil out of a drum set. Alex's hair was almost completely soaked with sweat and he had lost his shirt, which was seen dripping off the peg of a coat rack. I cringed at the thought of the certain smell of it. I waited til he finished his set, knowing he wouldn't hear me knock on the door, and watched his arms fly as I felt the vibration of the music in my feet from the floor. When I finally got his attention, he motioned me in.

"Hey," he breathed out heavily and guzzled half a bottle of water in one chug.

"Working hard, I see."

"Yeah, but it's break time anyway. I gotta get some food. You want to come with me?"

"Sure."

We headed back to the dining area. Alex splurged. He was taking full advantage of any benefits Reginald's gig offered him. He ordered cheese pizza, Chinese orange chicken and fried rice, hamburger steak, a tiny bit of spinach and greens, and a heaping pile of fluffy layered pudding dessert. I chose a grilled chicken salad, but couldn't resist a slice of pepperoni pizza.

Just as we had sat at a table, two veteran performers walked by and said, "Check it out. It's the rockstar." They mockingly threw up a rock fist.

"Oh, you're making friends too, huh?" I said.

"They're just mad that I took up one of the rooms they wanted."

"I have met several unfriendly faces today. Thank God for the girls and Zeke and Daniel… and you, I guess."

Alex smirked, "Speaking of the girls, I know you like Shay. What do you think of Ava?"

"She's nice. Little bit more energy than I'm used to. Like a cheerleader," I made an exaggeratedly excited face.

"Did she say anything about me?"

"Uh, she said it was sweet how nice you are to Daniel. Why?"

"She was eyeing me," he stated plainly.

"What? I don't think so."

"She was."

"She just broke up with some juggler Reginald axed. She's been talking all about it and how much she misses him," I said, trying to control my skepticism and surprise.

"So."

"So I don't think she was eyeing you." I emphasized the word eyeing.

"I bet you ten bucks she asks you about me by tomorrow," Alex's brow appeared determined.

"Fine. You're on."

He relaxed, popping his shoulders with a grin, and shoved another bite of pizza in his mouth.

"Anyway," I moved on, "the latest news is that Caroline saw my lyra practice and apparently this circus travels in ways other than via this ship."

"What does that mean?"

"Shay said she'll probably report to Reginald and maybe that's a good thing because he'll know I can do two apparatuses."

"No, I mean the travel."

"Oh. I don't know. Shay didn't elaborate."

"Well, you'll be fine with lyra. It suits you better than silks anyway."

"But I like silks and I've been working so hard."

"You'll do both, and it'll be great," he was somehow much less worried about my acts than any of the performers I had met today seemed to be. "How else can it travel from an island?"

"No idea."

We sat in comfortable silence for a while as Alex shoveled his food down. I ate my salad absentmindedly as I stared at the aerial apparatuses still hanging in our practice area. Glancing up and around the decks for signs of the Mandevilles.

"Shay says Caroline is the eyes and ears of this place. Told me to beware that she watches practices sometimes."

"I don't care if she watches me. I got nothing to hide."

I rolled my eyes, "How's the coaster progressing?"

"It's good. Apparently Reg is intrigued because he's had roustabouts working on it all day. Told me to make sure I check in and monitor the progress."

"You saw Reginald today?" I was somewhat in disbelief.

"Yeah, he stopped by during practice."

"And? How are you so relaxed about this?"

"Janie, we've been around his type before. He's intimidating you because you're letting him. I don't think he's that bad," Alex was finishing his hamburger steak and talking as nonchalantly as he would if it was about the weather forecast.

"I've heard a lot of stories in the past twenty-four hours. The consensus seems to be to watch out for him."

"Well, for now he's checking all the boxes for me. Pay, free food, nice sleeping quarters, funding the coaster."

"Just be careful," I said doubtfully.

As we finished eating, I thought about all the information I had heard so far about the Mandevilles and I felt resolute in the fact that they couldn't be trusted. But maybe Alex had a point. Maybe I needed to exude more confidence. Bullies tend to target the weaker ones, the ones who don't talk back or speak up. If the Mandevilles had a history of bullying their way to achieving the title of top traveling circus, they intended to keep that title and would do whatever was necessary to maintain it. I just hoped Alex would keep his eyes open and stay out of their crosshairs.

"I guess I'm going to get ready for an early night," I said.

"Me too, I'm beat. Plus, the boys kept me up late last night joking and telling stories."

"I'll see you in the morning then?"

"I'll be here for breakfast," he smiled and picked up his tray.

We walked together until the path split for men's and women's quarters.

"You know I've got your back, right?" Alex said before heading toward his room.

"Yeah, and ditto."

"Night."

Chapter 8

The Cube

The next morning came quickly, and I felt groggy and stiff as the sun peered through our small starboard side window. I could feel the subtle sway of the ship on the tides below us. Shay was milling around the room in her silk robe, getting ready for the coming practice. I could tell she was trying to be quiet for my sake.

"Morning, sunshine," she said as I rolled over, "you must've rested better because you weren't jabbering in your sleep."

"I guess," I swung my feet over the edge of the bed and sat upright, massaging my triceps and the backs of my knees. "I'm already sore from yesterday."

"Well then, boy do I have a treat for you." Shay spun to face me, silk robe floating and settling behind her. "I've given it some thought and I would like for you and I to do a doubles routine. Have you ever practiced lyra work on something other than a hoop?"

"No, but I've seen other routines on metal contraptions. Giant umbrellas, crescent moons, bird cages," I replied.

"I have an aerial cube. I've been waiting for an opportunity to use it in a show."

"Cube?"

"Yes. Did your math teacher ever show you how to draw a three-dimensional box on paper?"

"My math teachers were awful, or let's just say unaccommodating. But my grandpa showed me how to draw that when I was a kid."

"That's what it looks like. Only in metal," said Shay.

"Okay."

"I'm going to have the roustabouts bring it up from the cargo hold. So you better have a nice breakfast and do your yoga because I want to start today."

"You sure I'm up for this? You don't need to run this by the Mandevilles?" I asked.

"Let me worry about the Mandevilles. Just make sure to be ready for choreography at ten o'clock."

"Alright. I'll be there with bells on." I began my attempt to muster up the confidence that Alex had said I should have.

"Bells on?" Shay looked puzzled.

"Oh, sorry. That's just something my mother used to say all the time."

"Oh. Never heard that in Blue Smoke Bog. We have our own phrases too though."

"That's where you're from?" I asked Shay, intrigued by the name.

"Sort of." Shay's eyes looked thoughtfully at the ceiling. "That's a story for another time. I'm going to head to the wash room. See you at ten."

I thought to myself about what in the world a bog actually is. Was it like a swamp or a marsh? It was one of the type of places my travels hadn't landed me near so far. My lack of experience led me to think two lines of thought about swampy boggy places. That those places were where mystical magical things occur, or where you wind up dead because it was easier to hide bodies there. I really couldn't imagine someone as graceful and perfect as Shay in a place like that. But everyone has a story, and I continued to grow all the more fascinated by her's.

I arrived at the dining area thirty minutes earlier than our decided time of rendezvous. The cube was already suspended where the hoop had been rigged yesterday. It was significantly larger, to enable two people to pose on it rather than just one. I stared at it as I ate my eggs and turkey bacon, but I didn't feel nervous. I felt excited. Excited that Shay deemed me worthy to perform with her, excited to try a new apparatus.

Ava broke the line of positive self talk when she plopped in the seat next to me with her fruit and oatmeal.

"Morning, Janie. I see you guys broke out the cube."

"Shay's doings. I think we're going to choreograph a doubles routine today."

"That will be great! She's been talking about it over the past few months. I've seen her practice on it solo, but a doubles routine should impress the crowds even more."

"You think?"

"Crowds don't think about how hard performers train and work out choreography. How they religiously stretch to hit the most bendy poses. They just think the bigger the better."

"You're probably right about that."

"Regardless, it'll be great. You're in good hands with Shay," Ava patted my shoulder, "Anyway—you had a great practice yesterday, and I enjoyed meeting your friend."

"Thanks. It was more than I'm used to. Little sore today."

"Oh, you'll be fine. You get used to it. So, tell me about Alex."

There it was. I had lost the bet. How did he know? I thought about the smug look on his face when he said Ava was eyeing him. This was all so fun and easy for him, a dang joy ride pleasure cruise.

"What do you want to know?" I replied.

"Well, you guys are together, right?" Ava stated, as if she knew the answer had to have been yes.

"What? No, no. We're just friends."

Ava looked at me skeptically.

"Friends with benefits?" she pressed.

"No, definitely no," I said, looking down at my plate with wide eyes, as if I had just noticed something crawling on it.

"Come on, you can tell me. I won't say a word," Ava said.

I took a deep breath and looked at Ava, "Alex is my best friend. He's the only person that's been consistently in my life for the past few years. We have the same ideas about staying in one place, which is that it would be neither happy nor healthy for us."

"Well, I'd probably have to agree with you there. That's why I joined the troupe. My family runs a farm in a very small town, less than two thousand people. I thought to myself—be in one spot for my whole life? I couldn't bear the thought of being stuck there forever. There aren't enough people there for me to talk to. Much less find one to marry."

"You want to get married?" I asked tentatively.

Ava looked astonished, "Yeah, don't you?"

"I don't know. I haven't thought about it much. Wouldn't it be hard to be married while you're off with a circus?"

"Not if you marry someone who is a part of it," Ava said with a wink. "New performers are added to the show all the time. Granted, you have to watch out for the turnover. Look what it got me with my last beau."

"You miss him?" I asked.

"Eh, not really. Plenty of other fish in the sea. Oh, maybe we'll pick up a merman in Merdwick. That could be interesting," Ava shook her head back and forth as we laughed together at the thought.

"Seriously, though. You don't feel anything for Alex?" Ava laid down the final bit of the interrogation.

I answered her with a "no" quickly, but I had trouble getting my mind off the entire conversation. Because at this point, I couldn't imagine Alex not being around. Thankfully, Shay soon arrived and helped me get back on track to reclaim the morning.

After finishing breakfast, Ava headed off to her own practice and Shay and I stood by the cube, studying its structure. Shay already had ideas for two person poses. After another quick session of stretching, Shay inverted into the cube and positioned herself to one side of it. I watched her from the floor and she talked me through the poses as she transitioned through each of them.

"Let's work on these first few. So, get up here," she said encouragingly.

We worked through backbends positioned so that our heads hung outside the cube, splits within the cube at various angles, hanging from the top bars, and walking our feet in the air outside. All positions were contralateral and complimenting each other, almost as if mirroring the poses.

Shay's flawless beauty and flexibility was daunting to try to match. With each pose, she extended and flexed her legs and arms like a ballet dancer. Her hands softly floating through the cube, taking her arms to their next hold. She was my new role model, and though I wished I could be as beautiful as her, I felt overwhelmingly grateful just to be part of the art she was creating.

Her face appeared totally at ease, though I knew she was hiding the discomfort. The hard metal corners and edges were burrowing into her ribcage and back the same way it was mine. It was a great skill just to hide that fact. And though your skin gets tough and calloused, some poses will always be painful.

When we had finished going through the new choreography four times, we descended back to the floor. Shay still looked as pristine as she had this morning in her silk robe. I tried to feign energy and hide my fatigue, knowing the Mandevilles would constantly be on the look out, appraising performance and practices alike. Shay's example of maintaining poise consistently was a skill I knew I had to start working on.

"What do you think?" I asked her.

"I think we're on to something. I think we're off to a great start. And I also think we should try this performance out on the good people of Merdwick," Shay said confidently.

"Oh boy. You're serious?"

"Yep, I am."

I fought to keep up the confidence, and as I slowly sat down at a nearby table, I saw Alex walk through the entryway. Of course—he immediately went to the free food. When he looked my direction I waved a sarcastic salute. He made his way to the table and asked Shay if she would mind if he joined us.

"What's up? I like the new… thing you've got there," he asked, pointing at the cube.

"Aerial cube, you mean?"

"Obviously. Yes, the aerial cube," he said jokingly.

"We're doing a doubles routine, Shay and I."

"Very cool, very cool," he replied as he dove into his pile of snacks face first.

Shay laughed, "I'm going to get some fresh air. I'll catch up with you guys later," and she walked over to the glass elevator.

I threw ten bucks at Alex's side of the table.

"Surely you didn't lose the bet?" he said smugly.

"She did ask about you, so yes."

"What's that mean?" he asked.

"Doesn't matter, you won the bet," I stated flatly, to which he just shrugged and continued eating. "Speaking of," I trailed off when I noticed Ava coming to our table.

"Hey guys! How's it going?" Ava said as she sat down next to me.

"Pretty good. Shay wants to do the doubles routine in Merdwick. So I'm trying to psych myself up for that," I answered.

"That'll be great! Don't worry, Janie. I believe in you," she said, winking at me. "How are your practices going, Alex?" Ava asked.

"They're good. The roustabouts are putting the final touches on the drum coaster."

"Drum coaster?" Ava said.

"Oh yeah. You probably have no idea what I'm talking about. I'm a trick drummer. And I've had this roller coaster idea for it. Reg seems to think it'll be a hit, so I gave him the blue prints and he had it made," Alex said nonchalantly.

"Sorry, I'm still lost here," said Ava.

I watched him shoot her the half grin. The dreaded half grin. And I rolled my eyes at the sight of them dancing around each other's words carefully and anxiously. Alex put his food down and started using his hands to gesticulate the explanation.

"The drums are attached to a sort of car that moves along the track. It goes upside down, over the audience and everything. So I'll be strapped in and upside down and stuff." He started eating again, then looked at me and informatively stated, "we're test driving it this afternoon."

"It's happening!" I said in a funny voice about an octave higher than usual and assumed a faux surprised face. I was genuinely happy for him. He had wanted this for so long. Had droned on incessantly, talking about every detail for the past year. I just had mixed feelings about Reginald Mandeville being the one to orchestrate its creation.

"Wow," Ava breathed, "I've been doing this a while, and I've never seen anything like that before."

"Well, you could stop by and watch the test drive if you want. Janie you're coming, right?"

I hated that my stomach did a little backflip at the offer. Not to me, but to Ava. Part of me rationalized that this was no big deal. And another part of me feared all the what-if scenarios that my mind cooked up. What if Alex was tired of me? Following me to all the drab motels and scrounging for food and money. What if that was who I was to him? What if this was the beginning of the end of our friendship? I could come up with several movies where this near exact situation occurred.

"Janie, we should go," said Ava enthusiastically. Her blue eyes wide and framed with curling lashes. Her smile growing from small to huge, with her pearly teeth on exhibition. She pushed a section of light blonde hair behind her shoulder.

I couldn't decipher whether either of them truly wanted my accompaniment. And since I couldn't be sure, I came up with an excuse not to go.

"Well, actually I told Shay I would do a second practice this afternoon since she's ready to try the act. We arrive in Merdwick tomorrow night, so I don't have a lot of time."

Alex looked at me in disbelief. Maybe he did want me to come.

"I'm sorry, Alex. It's undoubtedly going to be amazing. I'll see it for the first time in the show, so that'll be all the better. Lights and roaring crowds."

"Janie's got a point. Last night before Merdwick. But I'll stop by if I get a break," Ava said to Alex with an encouraging smile.

"Alright. Whatever," Alex said. I watched his calm, flat expression and wondered if he honestly didn't care if either of us went. Maybe all of this was in my head.

"I'm gonna go track down Shay," I said, and dismissed myself from the table. I walked to the glass elevator and pushed the button to go up. Thankful that no one else was waiting for it, the doors slid open and I walked in. I had the whole thing to myself. As the elevator rose, I looked down at our table. Ava had stood up to go but was lingering, her arms crossed and her weight to the side on her left hip. She was laughing at something Alex said, and her hair swished as she giggled. I turned to watch the deck's railings instead.

I reached the top deck and walked straight out into the sun, toward the ship's port side railing. Breathing in the salty air and feeling the warm sun was the embrace I needed. It felt comforting and energizing to my sore muscles, and it lifted my mood. I had always felt solar powered. I looked out across the sea, watching it pass as we steadied ahead. Gulls were swinging and diving near the water's surface, looking for their own snacks.

The ocean has moods too. It can be a peaceful aesthetic or a lonely sight. Today it brought me peace, and I was thankful for it. It was times like these I thought Whisper must have known how I would be feeling that day, and painted a masterpiece to cheer me up. And ever the grand artist they were. The sky was periwinkle blue and punctuated with a few fluffy white clouds. Lit by the bright midday sun, the color of the ocean waves were more vibrant. It shown in variations of teals and cobalt blue, swirling amongst each other indicating the shallow and the great deep.

"Miss Morgan!" came a deep voice approaching from behind my right shoulder.

I turned around. Reginald walked up to the railing and propped his arms on them beside me, gazing out at the sea as I had done.

"Hello, Mr. Mandeville." I thought of Alex's advice, so I turned and positioned myself back on the railing same as Reginald. For a few seconds he said nothing. When he began to speak he kept his gaze forward on the ocean.

"Shay informs me you have other aerial experience and that the two of you are choreographing a duo performance for the first show."

"I believe that's the plan, sir."

"You know, I actually happened to see a bit of your practice today."

His voice was so calm and even that it felt eery, and I didn't like feeling that unbeknownst to me I had been watched.

"It wasn't bad. Caroline tells me that it appears you are working diligently during your practices. Perhaps it is paying off," said Reginald.

"Thank you, sir."

"Of course you'll have to keep it up. I expect my performers to remain sharp. And I must have perfection at the Merdwick show. Mr. Hagan has the fastest growing algae economy in the free world, and I am determined to procure a coveted role as shareholder. This circus doesn't run on hopes and dreams."

I didn't move a muscle, just continued to listen and occasionally glanced at him from the corner of my eye.

"I trust you'll do everything in your power to ensure your first performance is without error," Reginald spoke as he turned to face me. His voice cold and flat.

"I'll do my best," I responded, and with all the strength I could muster, I shifted and faced him. I looked at him as flatly and unemotionally as I could.

"Very well. Good day, Miss Morgan," he said, before turning and walking away.

I turned back toward the ocean and took some mindful breaths, mentally telling my shoulders to relax. Did Alex's advice actually work? Maybe the confidence thwarted Reginald after all.

I found Shay waiting at the elevator.

"Hey! So you talked to Reg?" I asked.

"Yeah, he caught me up here. Gave me the usual interrogation. But he seems to be on board with the duo routine."

"Would you mind if we had a second practice? Since we arrive in Merdwick so soon. I came up here to catch a breather and Reginald spoke to me too. Demanding perfection."

"What else is new?"

"He mentioned something about wanting to become a shareholder at that big algae company. So I guess we need to impress them," I added.

"Oh yes. The Mandevilles are always looking for more revenue." Shay's eyes scanned the top deck as we stepped in the elevator. She still lowered her voice, though it was only the two of us on it. "This isn't to be repeated. The Mandevilles have had great difficulty trying to conceive for the past couple of years. They've spent a fortune on fertility treatments, health related therapies, and diets.

Not to mention their typical lavish spendings on whatever they fancy at the time."

"Wow, I never would have thought," I said.

"It doesn't excuse all of their behavior, but it may explain some of it. Anyway, yes, we can run through the routine again this evening."

Shay and I took a break in the sauna before beginning a second practice. I was spent by the end, but started to feel more sure of myself. We refueled at dinner with grilled fish smothered in jerk seasonings, brussel sprouts roasted in honey, and wild rice. I could understand why Alex was so impressed with our meal benefits. I wondered why he hadn't beat us to the dining area.

After dinner, I left Shay and decided to check in on him. I stopped by the training rooms, but they were desolate by now, so I tried the top deck. He was on the same couch where we met the first night, kicked back and reading Limelight Drummer magazine. I bird whistled at him to get his attention. Recognizing the sound of it, he peeked over his magazine.

"You missed it. And it was awesome," he said, dropping his magazine on his chest. His eyes grew larger and he sat up, taking a deep breath; which I was certain would be followed by a lengthy monologue of the wonders that Reginald Mandeville had created for him. And as predicted, he spent the next fifteen straight minutes describing the first ride on the drum coaster bit by bit.

I was excited for him and felt a little guilty for skipping out. In spite of that, I justified it in my mind. I did need the extra practice. He didn't know that Reginald had approached and more or less threatened to oust me.

"Ava stopped by. Got to watch the tail end of it," Alex said.

"Oh. That's cool," I struggled to feign enthusiasm. "What'd she say about it?"

"Seemed pretty into it. She says it's not like any performance she has seen. Said the crowd should go nuts for it, especially the Marvelous Marvels fanbase. They'll be excited about something new."

"No doubt. I know it was amazing, even if I didn't see it," I said.

"What about you? How was the second practice?"

"Good, good. I'm feeling better about it." I noticed I was looking at my feet and worked to refocus on Alex's face. "Before we got started, I ran into Reginald. Or really, he ran into me. Actually, I think he intended to intimidate me into an ever growing allegiance to him."

"How did you handle it?"

"I used your advice. Play it cool, you know."

"What did he want?" Alex asked.

"He basically said that this show needs to be perfect because he wants to make a good impression on the CEO of the algae company. So he can become a shareholder."

"Interesting."

"Guess he thinks I'll screw it up. Wanted to remind me that if I did, I'll have to walk the plank," I said sarcastically, though wondering whether Reginald was really capable of such a thing. Was my dream a premonition?

"What a nice guy," Alex said mockingly. "Looking out for number one, I guess."

"Something like that, maybe," I said, thinking of number two being Caroline and number three being their potential offspring. Maybe I couldn't blame Reginald, were I in his shoes.

"Anyway," I shifted gears, "tomorrow will probably be a repeat of today, and then we dock at the port in Merdwick at night. Let's meet up before we disembark."

"Sounds good."

I stood up and looked over the top deck. Above us, the sky was purplish black again; with white dots of stars sprinkled across it. I enjoyed how quiet and expansive it felt at sea. How it was off the grid. It was nice since we were about to be smack in the middle of hordes of people. Despite the stress bestowed on to me by the Mandevilles, I had grown quickly comfortable aboard the *Light Catcher.*

After I left Alex, I headed down the glass elevator and through the hallways to mine and Shay's room. It took me much longer to fall to sleep. Instead, I laid there looking at the shred of moon light that passed through our small window and onto the floor of wooden boards. Paying attention to the feeling of the ship's sway as I lay still. Enjoying it for one more night.

I thought of Whisper and asked to get through this first performance unscathed, but I finally drifted into soft unconsciousness as I tried to finish a sentence.

Merdwick

I started the morning by carrying out the same routine as I had on our first day of conditioning, plus meticulous practice of our new doubles routine on the cube. I kept at it throughout the day, even without Shay to counterbalance. And must've worked through our routine fifteen times.

During the first duo practice with Shay, I saw Caroline walking along the railing a few floors above us. I knew she was keeping tabs on us, but didn't think much of it. I was already trying my hardest to execute positions with grace, point my toes, arch my back, float my arms, and keep my face composed. And regardless, Caroline never directly acknowledged us.

We all ate dinner together. The girls at one table and the boys at the table next to us. And then we parted ways to pack our belongings and ready ourselves to disembark. I didn't have much to pack, so I finished quickly. I gave a final glance around the little room Shay and I had shared, taking in the first part of the journey, and walked out.

As I ambled through the ship and up to the top deck, I found the hallways were extra busy. Performers, roustabouts, and the ship's staff were buzzing about. Crossing rooms and hallways was trickier, and the senior performers most certainly didn't make way for the new girl.

At the top deck, I sat in the usual chairs and watched the sun begin to sink. What started as light pink and soft orange skies leisurely deepened into hues of magenta, fuchsia, and violet. Alex appeared as they were evolving into a more indigo and navy color.

We sat and took it in. There's nothing like a sunset at sea, a vivid and striking masterpiece in the sky. The vastness of it envelopes you. It reminds you that you're small, and that thankfully there is something greater that is in control.

"A sunset like this must be a good sign," said Alex.

"Hopefully. Have you heard what time we should arrive?"

"Zeke said he heard that it should be around eight o'clock. So we've got about thirty minutes if that's right." Alex moved his bag to the floor and kicked his feet up. "Hey! Aren't we supposed to be guarding ourselves from vicious spear throwing water people? We should be trespassing into their territory soon."

"*Shhhhh*. Some people really seem to believe that stuff, and I don't need another reason for someone to dislike me. Everyone always hates the doubters in scenarios like that."

"I didn't tell you Daniel's story. Remember when I mentioned it to Shay? He said he's seen one?"

"Yeah."

"He saw one in Caroline's former circus, Zingo's Symposium Of The Strange. He said they had a mermaid in a large clear tub, on display for the show. Sounds like it was just a girl in a suit, but you know Daniel. He takes things at face value."

"Did Daniel come from Zingo's?" I asked.

"I guess so," Alex shrugged.

"Interesting. I figured Mr. Mandeville would not be a fan of Daniel's, but then again I guess Caroline seems a little softer," I pondered.

"I think Daniel is kind of scared of Reginald. His eyes dart if Zeke or I mention his name," Alex replied.

"Poor guy," I thought of how easy it would be for Reg to intimidate Daniel, to crush his beautiful spirit. The thought of anyone bullying Daniel set my insides aflame. And it only made me despise Reg all the more.

"You need to watch out for him. If you can," I said to Alex.

"I know. Zeke and I are trying. Daniel says he likes us much better than his last roommates," Alex laughed.

"Good. How's Zeke doing?"

"He's ready to get off the boat. To see the new digs. See where they plan to put Tombo."

I stood and walked to the railing to check if I could see anything. Alex followed suit. It was quiet on the top deck now. I assumed everyone was heading to the bottom floors to scramble for who gets off the gangway first. Alex and I scanned the dark line that separated water and air.

"We've made it this far together. I hope I can keep up with you," I said to Alex.

"What do you mean?"

Turning a little to face him, "They're going to love your show. You're set. I can't mess up or they'll leave me in Merdwick," I said.

"We're not splitting. I saw the duo routine. Shay's got you. Stop worrying," Alex said as he slung his left arm around my shoulders and shook me until I smiled.

"Check it out," said Alex, pointing toward the emerging silhouette of buildings on a shoreline. "Reminds me of our beach days."

It was dark now, and a fog had settled near the shore, making it difficult to determine the structures lining it. Lights from the buildings were blurred in the mist, dulling their yellow glow. And the current perspective gave the first glance, at what would be our home for the next several days, an eerie tone.

We drew nearer, and the city became more visible. One could see large architecture towards the west end of the city, much taller than any of the surrounding buildings, and I assumed it might be the algae company. Straight ahead were humbly sized houses. And to the east was another large structure, almost cathedral like. The top of it bordered with several peaked roofs. *Light Catcher* began slowly gliding toward it.

I looked at the sea beneath us. No signs of merpeople, but a substantial amount of jelly fish bobbed just under the surface, the scarce light reflecting their bulbous bodies iridescently. They floated in all directions, dragging long curly and cotton looking tentacles in their wake. The thought of swimming through their midst made me cringe at the certain painful and potentially paralyzing fate it would bring to a human being. I pointed them out to Alex, but he quickly returned his gaze forward.

"We're headed straight for it," he said, pointing ahead. "Looks like there's some sort of entry in the center."

I strained and squinted my eyes to see. It was an enclosed docking or mooring edifice in which you steered your vessel inside of. A large boat drifted out of the entry and veered towards the west as we approached.

Framing the open sea entrance were two statues that I could now make out the details of. They were fitting to the stories I had been told ever since I first heard the name Merdwick. The statue on the right was a kingly looking man with a swirling beard and holding a three-pronged trident, pointed toward the center peak of the entryway as if guarding it. It bore a crown on its head and its lower body was that of a scaled fish's tail; essentially some sort of merman. The statue on the right was female. Its head was held high and its chest pushed up and forward. It too held a spear angled forward in front of its body, with the sharp pointed end toward the sea. However, its lower body was that of an octopus. The tentacles separately spaced apart but positioned almost in the shape of a ball gown, tapered toward the bodice but wide at the hem.

The *Light Catcher*, though massive, passed easily between them and into what looked like a channel. Slowing to a very slight drift, we continued until we reached an unusual looking dock on our starboard side.

"I guess we should head down," I said.

Alex and I took the usual route. Glass elevator to the open deck at the stern. The mass of people from our troupe and crew were steadily making their way forward, bottle necking to get over the gangway. I could see Shay and Ava near the front of the crowd, and Zeke and Daniel a couple rows behind them.

Once you passed over the gangway, you had to proceed through an extraordinarily housed gate. To reach it, you had to walk through an anglerfish statue. Its long pointy teeth framed the edge of the entry and its eyes shimmered a dark green. The only light leading you through it, of course, was the spherical orb hanging like a lantern over its head and in front of its mouth. Anglerfish use this to lure in prey, and the metaphor of it all had my head spinning and heart rate slightly increased.

Alex and I neared the gateway. "I don't know about you, but I feel very relaxed," I said to Alex sarcastically.

"They love their sea creatures and folk lore around here," he replied while gazing at the lure and teeth of the statue with a look of hubristic incredulity on his face.

Everyone stopped just beyond the gateway, a mass of performers dressed in every color of the rainbow, toting suitcases and pulling along various circus accoutrements. Together we stood before a tall skinny man in a shabby pageboy style cap, suspenders, and holding a tall shepherd's hook with a lantern atop it. He looked a little miffed to be tasked with guiding our crowd.

"Welcome Marvelous Marvels," he stated flatly as his blank eyes scanned left to right. "I am Mr. Habbershack and I am hotelier at Seafarer's Cove. Now, a few things you need to know about Seafarer's Cove. It is a channel that goes completely through the structure you are standing in now," he gestured to our left where boats were slowly going in and out. "However, if you walk along this path towards the back wall, you cannot see the throughway beneath the surface. That is unless tides are extremely low, and they haven't been low in all the years I've been here. Please refrain from venturing near the back wall as we are undergoing some maintenance." Alex and I looked at each other with suspicion. Mr. Habbershack continued, "I will now escort you to the cove lodgings."

Mr. Habbershack turned and led us further into the cove, his lantern jostling and swinging with his gait. In the dim lighting I saw that the cove itself was constructed of stone, and it felt sort of like a medieval castle, drafty and damp. The scratchy shuffle of everyone trudging along the way indicated moisture on the floor, condensation and the remnants of the path sailors had trod.

Encapsulated by the crowd, we could now longer see the channel to our left. But the lapping of the water against the barnacle laden sides of it could be heard sporadically.

Looking ahead, I saw light emanating from an opening to our right. As Alex and I neared, and the crowd began to enter, we got a view of a hallway entrance. It was framed by ten foot tall sea horse statues. Both pointing their snouts toward the opening as if keenly occupied by watching the comings and goings there.

We turned and walked through the sea horses' guard into a brighter and more inviting entry way; to my relief. Shells and sea glass were inlaid on the stones, some of which flickered as it reflected the glowing lantern. Every fifteen feet or so, there were elaborate wall sconces crafted to look like coral colored octopus tentacles holding large yellow bulbs. I began to get excited about the look of our lodging.

Mr. Habbershack had stopped at a crossroads of hallways, "Women's lodgings are to the left, men to the right. You'll find a posted list of your rooms pinned temporarily, just there," he pointed to the front of each entry, "and if you continue further in, you'll find the land entrance." He pointed behind him to the door, "There is a restaurant and pub conveniently nearby called The Old Seawitch." And with that Mr. Habbershack excused himself.

The crowd of men and women separated like oil and water. It would be interesting being in the same hall as the men, able to see them enter and exit their rooms. I scanned the list to find that Shay, Ava, and I were sharing one of the first rooms in the women's hall.

When I opened the door to our room, Shay and Ava were already inside. The room itself was mushroom shaped, a short hall-like entry and a curving wall that three beds fanned across. I was unsettled by the fact that there weren't any windows. I knew that would catalyst a quick onset of cabin fever. But despite that significant complaint, the room was spotless, updated, and on theme with the decor. There were octopus tentacles everywhere. Holding up furniture, sprawled across the headboards, and curling around to form a grand chandelier in the middle of the room. I was also excited to find we had our own bathroom. Though I was a little apprehensive about sharing it with two women, having roomed with Alex for so long.

"We're all together this time!" Ava appeared hopeful for a full on nightly slumber party. "Isn't the room cool?"

I put my bag on the empty bed, "It's beautiful, but a little confining without a view out."

"Yeah, I don't like that either," said Shay as she arranged the clothes inside her suitcase. "I need some nature nearby."

"You've got sea life," Ava said sarcastically, pointing at the octopus chandelier.

Shay raised an eyebrow at her and said nothing. I was thankful she would be around to even out the energy levels our three personalities had.

"Land, Sea, Sky. None of it visible in here. I guess we'll have to wait for morning to see that," said Shay.

"I can't wait that long. So I guess I'll go look at the sea in the channel tonight before bed," I said.

"Ew, it's dark and sticky and damp. And it smells funny," said Ava.

"Water calms me," I replied, shrugging.

I didn't bother unpacking my stuff, that would have taken about two seconds considering how minuscule the quantity of my stuff was. Instead, I told the girls I'd be back shortly and headed out the door.

When I arrived back at the hallway crossroads, I saw Alex about to enter his room, which was not far down the men's hallway.

"Hey! I'm heading back to explore if you wanna join," I called.

"Meet you there," he replied as he heaved his duffle bag through the doorway.

I kept walking back toward the channel, stopping along the hallway to look more closely at the tiny cone, scallop, and clam shells scattered within the stones. I ran my fingers across the tentacle sconces. Walking toward the sea entrance at night was like walking toward a great black void. I imagined that, during the day, light could make its way into the some of the cove, but at night it felt eerie. Especially as I left the warm glow of our hallway.

Very few people were traversing the docks. There were wooden benches bolted to the ground near the ledge that guarded pedestrians from the lip of the channel. I plopped down on one and stared at the water.

Out the mouth of the great cove entrance, I could see the fog had now settled. Moonlight and a few lanterns were the only instruments of visibility, and they were scarce. I couldn't even make out the once flamboyant *Light Catcher*. Maybe she was shut down or moved to a different docking area now that the troupe had abandoned her.

I slumped into the bench trying to get slightly more comfortable and watched the tiny shreds of moonbeams reflect on the billowing channel.

I had just started to relax when I felt two large hands quickly press down on my shoulders and an odd squawking scream.

"Son of a…," I huffed and jolted myself upward.

Alex guffawed, holding his ribs with one arm. He curved around the bench and dropped himself beside me.

"I thought you were Miss Billie Badass," he teased.

I shook off the unpleasant tingling of my nerves. "Just trying to keep up with you, hot shot. But even you can admit it's a little creepy in here."

"Eh, ambiance of the rugged lives of drunken sailors," he said quietly through closed teeth, so that if one was around, they couldn't hear him. "Feels manly to weather the elements. Do without the joys of modern electricity," he sunk into the bench, crossing his arms.

We both stared at the channel for a while, watching a few boats slowly move back and forth through murky waters, in and out of port. I wondered why the one's going out of the cove were leaving. Where were they headed? Night fishing or maybe checking crab traps? Alex crossed his arms behind his head and laced his fingers.

"What's the plan for tomorrow?" he asked.

"Dunno, I'm hoping Shay will lead the way. May go to the pub tomorrow night. Looks like there's no glorious dining area here," I replied.

"We're supposed to get paid after the first show. Until then, it may be hard to cover meals at the pub."

"I've got a little. Meet me there and I'll spot you. I owe you anyway," I said.

"For what?"

I turned to give him a face of defeat in autonomy yet genuine gratefulness, "for general support, advice on handling Reg, and decent friendship."

"True," Alex nodded as he stared at his feet. He looked up at the sound of something plunging into the water.

A boat had stopped and nestled into a port far into the cove on the other side of the channel, where it was dark and away from most docks; a good distance past the bench we sat on. Men were trudging along the sides and dragging nets over the railing. It was hard to make out in the dark, but it seemed there was no movement in the nets. And yet, they appeared full.

"What's in the nets?" I said under my breath, more to myself than to Alex.

"Probably fish, dummy," Alex said nonchalantly.

"No," I elbowed him, "It's not moving."

In the dim shreds of light, I could see him squint at the boat. I turned to keep watching. The boat had one lantern on the side of the ship and I strained my eyes around it. The crew was emptying the nets now, but they weren't moving quickly. Like they would if they were catching stray flopping fish, or trying to grab one from mid air after it slips out of their hands; like those slippery water tube toys that you can't hold without it rolling out of your grasp.

As I was watching the crew, I noticed a subtle shift in the water near the stern. I tapped Alex's knee and pointed that direction. Quietly, a beige looking blob was rising just a few inches above the water, then sinking back down again.

We didn't say a word, watching it almost breathlessly. For the next five minutes, the crew continued glumly trudging back and forth dragging lifeless nets, and the blob kept discreetly breaking the surface.

"What the heck is that?" I whispered to Alex, without moving any muscles in my face or body.

He followed, "I don't know. Probably just a buoy."

The crew was finishing up, and a man started walking toward the stern. He looked around the cove and I got the sudden feeling that I needed to hide. Like I was about to witness something I shouldn't. I doubted he could see us in the darkness, but slumped further down on the bench, pulling Alex down with me.

I guess I was right because the man looked satisfied and dropped something small off the stern into the water.

Right before it hit the surface, the beige blob rose and I saw what looked like a hand reach up out of the water. Then it slowly sank beneath the cover of the channel.

"What the—," Alex breathed.

I felt my whole body shiver and the sensation of someone walking up behind me in the dark. I never really loved the dark anyway and now I felt vulnerable to it. Were our minds playing tricks on us?

The fearful response made me instinctually cling to Alex. And he must've felt funny too because he pulled me up and drug me to the furthest wall from the channel, back towards our lit hallway.

"What did you see?" I asked as we entered. Alex's eyes were wide but topped with heavy, scrunched eyebrows. I knew he was still processing what we'd just seen. He didn't speak for a second.

"I'm not sure. What did you see?"

"I asked you first," I hissed.

"Well, there was something in the water," he stated blankly.

"Ya think!?" At least he admitted that much. "Ugh, I'll never sleep," I huffed.

"Maybe it was a buoy."

"I thought I saw a hand," I said with anxiety.

Alex's eyes darted around, "That's crazy. We just couldn't see."

"Then why did you jump up so quickly?"

"I dunno. Maybe we just need to stay out of the cove at night. We know nothing about the people here."

"I've heard a little," I huffed.

"That stuff is probably lore. This is the site of a huge lucrative algae industry. The head honcho of this thing may run it by illegal means. I don't think it would be in our best interest to witness something we weren't meant to see."

I could see that Alex was convincing himself in his mind. He would not entertain the idea of merpeople. And ordinarily I wouldn't have either, but now I was getting the heebie jeebies.

"Alright, well what should we do?" I asked.

"Just go to bed. Don't talk about it to anyone."

I took some deep breaths, and we walked back towards our halls.

"I'll see you tomorrow. Get some sleep," Alex said.

"Alright. Night," I replied and turned to go to my room. I didn't really want to be away from Alex. Just the thought of faking calm with the girls had me exhausted already.

I opened the door to our room and found Ava reading a magazine and Shay with her nose in a book about plants for herbalist or botanists.

"Feeling relaxed now?" Ava asked.

"Yep, off to bed for me," I said, trying not to make eye contact with either of them. I went straight to the bathroom, closed the door, and slapped some water on my face from the faucet. I noticed the water had a unique smell to it. Shaking it off, I put on my pajamas and looked in the mirror. I closed my eyes and focused on breathing in and exhaling out for a minute. Trying to calm down before going back out.

As I got into bed I nonchalantly commented, "The water smells funny."

"I know," Shay's voice trailed, and she didn't look up from her book, "it's some sort of plant smell. I'm trying to place it."

"Seaweed?" I asked.

"Maybe."

"Well, goodnight ladies," I flopped into bed and rolled to face the corner away from them and their lamps.

I stared at the wall, thinking about the blob and the hand. It took a while for my eyes to become heavy. When I drifted to sleep, I dreamt that the man on the boat used a spotlight to check the cove. The beam blinded my eyes as it stopped its oscillating movements on me and Alex.

My body jerked, waking me temporarily, but thankfully I fell back asleep.

Chapter 10

The Fairgrounds

In the morning, I woke up feeling wretched. I had wakened in the night more than once, and must've grinded my teeth because my jaw was sore. The girls were milling about the room, getting ready for the day. I jumped out of bed and hit the shower, grateful for its convenient location and that the water was still warm. Knowing that the humidity of this place would do nothing for my hair, I piled it on top of my head in a curly wad of a bun. I threw on my active wear, swished the mascara wand through my eyelashes, brushed my teeth, and emerged from the bathroom.

"Did you know you grind your teeth at night?" Ava asked.

"Uh, yeah, sometimes I do that," I said.

"I bet you're hurting today. Bad dreams?" Ava looked at me like a nursemaid trying to pinpoint the trigger of an ailment.

"Oh. Nah. Just jitters from wondering what the new place will be like. You guys know where we are practicing?"

"Evidently Mr. Habbershack is escorting us to the fairgrounds, which is where we will practice and perform. There's a large building there, where they have community events," Shay said.

"Escorting us how?" asked Ava.

"I have to assume by boat for our lot," Shay replied.

I didn't like the thought of going to the channel again. Stepping over that murky water, even if over a gangway. It was daunting, and I tried to suppress any look of dread or apprehensiveness. I hoped it was a bright sunny day because I wanted visibility.

When we stepped out of our room, it was loud and crowded as the troupe was packed into the hallway. There were performers chattering everywhere about routines, tricks, who was going to furnish breakfast, and how they were tired of travel by boat. I wedged in between Big Bertha, the two ton lady, and the snake charmer who was carrying a straw basket at her waist line that I prayed was secured shut. Shay and Ava huddled in as well.

Trying to relax in the commotion, I looked down the men's hall. I saw Zeke holding the carrier case, that undoubtedly held Tombo, bear hugged to his chest. He looked exhausted already. Next to him, Daniel merely smiled his huge toothy grin, happily amongst the troupe. Seeing his happy face gave me a sense of calm. I could see the top of Alex's tousled hair behind them, but he was obscured from view.

Mr. Habbershack moseyed up to our congregation and led us back towards the channel. As we filed out of our hallways, the girls and I ended up in line near the boys. I inconspicuously shot Alex a look. He bounced his eyebrows once in recognition.

It wasn't as eerie in the channel entry of the cove since I was surrounded by our entire circus. But though it was a perfectly clear day with no rain, the grayish white skies did little to improve visibility. I could see all the boats swaying idly at each dock, and the empty bench where I had witnessed the blob. The channel's green hue reflected against the interior stone walls. Gulls were swooping and darting in the sky just beyond the entrance.

What I could not see was *Light Catcher*. I scanned the great domed building left and right, but saw no sign of her. And as I thought about her absence, I realized I hadn't seen the Mandevilles in a while. Where was our fearless leader?

I exhaled a whistle that Alex would recognize. He looked back at me over his shoulder. "Where's *Light Catcher*?" I mouthed silently to him.

He couldn't read my lips because he mouthed, "What?"

"Where's *Light Catcher*?" I repeated with animated emphasis.

The second time Shay noticed me and said, "You okay, Janie?"

"What? Oh yeah. I just didn't see our ship," I replied abruptly.

"Oh. Yes, *Light Catcher* is probably gone."

"What? Why? How will we get off this island?" I stuttered.

"I told you. This circus travels by other modes of transportation. Don't worry about it now. It's fine. Relax."

Shay truly was relaxed, though I couldn't understand how she could be. In this damp, smelly sea town having to place full faith in Mr. Habbershack that we make it across waters infested by who knows what, to some port for a big time CEO Alex seems to think could be a criminal. When she continued, I felt like she could see what was in my head.

"I have on good authority that Mr. Habbershack has been doing this a while. They have events here all the time since the algae boom. This is the usual routine for people who travel in to attend parties, seminars, fundraisers."

We continued forward, following the troupe ahead, and I watched as Zeke, Alex, and Daniel passed over the gangway onto the boat that would take us out. They were fine, so I tried to relax. When we got to the edge of the dock, I stepped up the gangway. I looked through the rough aluminum slats into the water as I walked. Just before I took my first step onto the boat, I thought I saw an iridescent shimmer flash through the water. It startled me, and I leapt awkwardly onto the deck.

A couple performers turned to look at me since my landing made a racket.

"She's scared of water. Can barely swim," Alex offered the rash explanation to those looking. He grabbed my arm roughly and yanked me out of the way.

"OW!"

"Keep it together," he said through closed teeth, "sorry."

He frowned as I rubbed my arm. Our two groups settled together near the bow. The boat tediously made way out of Seafarer's Cove and into open water. Dull skies, and the sun covered by overcast, made the sea appear even more dark and murky. The aesthetics did not inspire any positive feelings about what the actual city of Merdwick might be like.

I saw a glimpse of Tombo through the star cut outs on Zeke's carrier, which reminded me of the rest of the animals. That led me to wonder what conditions they were housed in at the fairgrounds. And how did Zeke get Tombo into the cove anyway?

"Good day, Marvelous Marvels. This is Mr. Habbershack speaking. I am to brief you all on the history of Merdwick and your agenda for today," came a voice over an intercom.

Our group exchanged scattered looks at each other until all the pairs of eyes found rest in a gaze over the horizon and our ears took charge. Mr. Habbershack continued his narration.

"Merdwick, once known as a humble fishing town, became sensationalized six years ago by a marine biologist who frequented the area claiming to research water properties and marine behavior patterns. He discovered that properties of our algae and seaweed could be used to make fuel. But what he really nosed in to research was more than common sea life." There was a pause and a muffled interjection from whoever else was in the room with Habbershack.

"Anyway—," the intercom lecture continued, "Around that time, Mr. Hagan, CEO of Green Vitality Incorporated, caught wind of it and settled here. He's created one of the largest algae harvesting businesses in the world. Had the fairgrounds built shortly afterwards to house events to raise money," and he mumbled, "Like he doesn't have enough."

By now we were venturing closer to the shore line towards a small marina. Saw palmettos and longleaf pines fringed the edge of the coast, an occasional palm tree here and there placed to create a welcome atmosphere. Next to the marina was a fairly large building with a sign across the top in curling typeface that read *Merdwick Fairgrounds*.

"You Marvels will trek from the marina to the fairgrounds. Breakfast is supplied for you there. You will have until five o'clock to practice, or do whatever it is you do, and be back at the marina. If you want to sleep in your room at the cove, that is."

I could see, as always, Alex was delighted by the promise of free food. He also looked very entertained by Mr. Habbershack's unfiltered commentary.

"The animals are housed in the barn behind the fairgrounds. We're not responsible for transporting them to the fairgrounds, so you're on your own there."

We docked and the troupe began shuffling about, picking up their things and heading towards the exit. It was then that I noticed a face I hadn't seen in a while,

Anthony's. He was back towards the helm, completely dressed to the nines, scribbling in a small notebook that he propped against a dirty old cooler.

"Shay, what is Anthony's role in the circus?" I asked, nodding towards his direction.

"Assistant to the Mandevilles."

"Where are the Mandevilles?" I prodded.

Shay gave me a bit of a teasing look, "How should I know?"

"Well, you seem to know everything," I said.

"She does. Don't let her fool you," Ava interjected.

Shay rolled her eyes at us, "Well if he's here," she glanced at Anthony, "then they most likely have already been to the city for their own purposes."

We were going to be the last bunch off the boat, so we made our way to the exit. Anthony had finished whatever it was he was writing and tucked the notebook in his breast pocket. Since his role was new information to Alex, Zeke, and myself, we all but curtsied to him, smiling and nodding to him like a mischievous band of fifth graders to a teacher. He responded with what looked like a genuinely warm smile and extended a hand to beckon us to exit before him. Zeke was particularly clumsy since he was trying to divert attention from Tombo, but he also seemed a little struck by Anthony's perfectly symmetrical facial structure.

We walked across the gangway and I inspected the water beneath but saw nothing. The marina was obviously updated, but I could tell that it was modest upon construction. We followed the troupe up the boardwalk and along a pathway amongst the palmettos that led to the fair grounds. The howl or bellow of a circus animal in the barn behind it could be heard intermittently as we approached.

Once inside the building on the fairgrounds, where we would perform our show for two nights, we found there was really nothing to write home about. It had a great open floor area smack in the center of it and seating on all sides. In its vacant state it felt bleak and desolate. White walls and empty chairs.

Reginald and Caroline entered from a side door, at a brisk pace, with a goal oriented look in their eyes.

"Alright, crew. First show is tomorrow evening," Reginald's voiced boomed and echoed in the building. "Mr. Hagan has had this date set for a month and people have already arrived on the island. You will have all of today at your disposal to ensure that routines are perfected, and by tomorrow I expect them to be flawless. Is that clear?"

The entire group answered an affirmative, "Yes, sir." Adults answering like they had been enlisted in the army. I wondered what we had gotten ourselves into.

"There will be an additional side show," Reg continued. I noticed Big Bertha's eyes dart to Master Kai, the strong man. "It will be presented tomorrow. And I don't want any of my troupe making a fuss about it. Keep your mouth shut and mind your own performances."

And with that Reg gave us all a quick fake smile and turned on his heel to exit from where he came. Caroline took a soft, graceful step forward.

"Breakfast is in the adjoined building, compliments of Mr. Hagan. He has catered lunch as well, but you will be responsible for dinner. Rigging attachments are in place for all aerialists. There will be a separate tent beside the main entryway for side show act performances before and after the main show. If you work with animals, you are solely responsible for all of their care and transport to and from this building." She gave a polite nod as she pulled out her cigarette holder, "Happy practicing."

We all watched Caroline float out after Reginald, and then everyone made their way toward free breakfast. It was quite a spread, though I'm sure it was pennies to Mr. Hagan if he was anywhere near as wealthy as I kept hearing. Mountains of pancakes and waffles, giant trays of sausage and bacon, bowls piled high with hard boiled and scrambled eggs. Every fruit you could imagine was on display and arranged neatly in the shape of a tropical fish on a huge platter.

Alex was overly excited and repeatedly reported to all who would listen, "this is even better than the meals on *Light Catcher*."

As I sat down at a table beside Shay, I scanned the buffet area. I watched as Daniel was rooted out of the way, from his spot in the line, and made to wait on several performers. My jaw clenched. People were always taking advantage of him or disregarding him completely. I grew more and more angry as I observed, but Daniel remained smiling. How did he do that? How did people do that to him?

"It kills me how people trample on Daniel," I said when Shay gave me an inquisitive look.

"I know," Shay answered quietly. "I hate it too. But I think Daniel is thrilled to be a part of the circus. You know how he got here?"

"No," I gruffly answered as I kept my eyes on his bright eyed grin, watching others pass in front of him, ignoring his generous yield.

"It was all Caroline."

"Caroline? Really?"

"He came with her from Zingo's. He was just a clown there. And Reginald was not on board with taking him in, but she convinced him that Daniel could do more than clown entertainment. Got him in front of Reginald's largest prize, Eloise, which he hijacked from another dying circus. Eloise sealed the deal. Took to Daniel instantly. Followed him everywhere."

"Wow. Wouldn't have guessed that," I lowered my voice and leaned in towards Shay, "So Caroline's not so bad as Reginald?"

"I don't know about all that. Don't underestimate her. She can be tolerant, but she values perfection in this circus as much, if not more, than Reg does. And she may do whatever it takes to ensure it. Remember Ava's juggler beau?"

"Easy for her. She's naturally so beautiful. And all she has to do is float around assisting the ringmaster."

"Caroline performs."

"She does?"

"Yes, she's a renowned contortionist," Shay said enthusiastically.

Zeke plopped down beside us with his tray. "Ladies," he greeted us, "you guys talking about the dear ol' Mandevilles?"

"Janie didn't know Caroline was a contortionist."

Zeke looked at me puzzled, "Yes, you did. I told you at the cafe."

"Yeah, I just thought she no longer performed. I never saw her practicing anywhere on the ship. How do you know so much about their history?" I asked Zeke, trying to counter their disbelief at my lack of knowledge in the chronicles of Marvels.

"I've been following them since I was a kid. Carlyle's Carnival Of Wonders was the first circus I ever visited," he answered, and began munching on some fruit from his plate.

"Anyway," Shay continued, "Caroline performs. So does Reg."

"He still swallows swords?" I assumed that Reginald no longer felt obligated to perform since he was the all powerful king of this entire circus.

"Oh yeah," answered Zeke, "He's amazing. Holds the current world record for the longest sword swallowed. Two feet of thick steel in your gut."

"Am I sensing a fanboy?" I winked at Zeke.

"Alright, I confess. I know they're a little shady, but I'm a huge fan," Zeke said, almost apologetically to Shay. "You gotta take the good with the bad, right?" he said.

"True."

"What I want to know is the scoop on Anthony. I know nothing about him or his role here," Zeke added. "He seemed to have some weight in whether I made it through auditions. And he's always scribbling in that little book."

"Assistant to the Mandevilles," I added an upturn at the end of my statement and glanced at Shay like I was trying to remember the answers to pass a quiz in grade school.

"Yes," she said. "He's an assistant and talent scout."

"Well, he's talented at fashion and grooming. Easy on the eyes," said Zeke.

"Oh, you think so," Shay teased.

"Side sweep and stubble. Yes," Zeke was gazing at the ceiling in pleasant thought until he sort of snapped out of it, "But what you said earlier on the boat—are you saying he's a spy?"

"I don't know. He's a paid assistant," Shay shrugged.

I was giggling at Zeke when I saw Alex making his way to our table with a mountain of food unlike any I had seen him lugging before. Two plates and a cup held in his teeth. Zeke pushed a chair out for him. He sat down and immediately started digging through the piles, and we all stared for a full minute before he noticed we were gaping at him.

"What?"

"Good morning, pig," I said.

"Hey, I burn a lot of energy drumming," he justified and kept eating.

It was true. For all the food he ate, it didn't seem to go anywhere. He remained slim and shredded from all the thrashing about he did while slamming hard plastic drum heads.

"We were just talking about this Anthony character," Zeke said.

Alex paused for two seconds, raised an eyebrow, and cast a knowing glance at Zeke. Then kept on eating.

"Sorry to change the subject, but what's the plan for today? I gotta get with it if the first show is tomorrow," I said.

"We'll practice the doubles routine, break, stretch, repeat, ferry back. We're on our own for dinner, so I vote the pub," said Shay.

"I bet we'll fit in well with the patrons that frequent The Old Seawitch," Zeke grimaced as he rolled his eyes.

Chapter 11

The Old Seawitch

Practice went relatively smooth, despite the fact that it was our first time at the new venue. I envisioned the actual performance taking place as I went through our choreography. I imagined the warm glow of the light show in reds, blues, and violets. The smell of neon pink cotton candy and buttery popcorn. The sounds of gasps and applause at the poses and flips Shay and I would do as we spun in the air.

As usual, I was exhausted by the end of the day, but felt fairly confident about my first performance with the Marvelous Marvels. I was actually relieved to be performing the doubles routine on the cube, rather than the silks routine as I initially thought. It felt less alone, less sink or swim, to have a partner.

The troupe footed back to the marina as the sun was setting. All day it had been dark and gloomy—I struggled to prevent it from zapping my energy. Yet in the afternoon, the sun finally appeared just before it settled beneath the horizon.

It cast shades of red, gold, and yellow over the sea. I took it as a good sign. There was a saying that went 'red sky at night, sailors delight.' And though none of us were sailors, everyone seemed to enjoy the ferry ride back to Seafarer's Cove thanks to the pleasing aesthetic.

When we arrived to the channel of the cove, docked, and got off the ferry, I was so jittery about the first show being within twenty-four hours that I didn't really think about the blob. Shay and Ava insisted on showering before dinner. And Daniel was assisting Zeke, who had again somehow managed to bring Tombo back to the cove and needed to get him settled in the boys' room. Alex's priority was food, so he and I dumped our stuff and headed out. Lots of performers shuffled along the hallway and through the land entrance door in hopes that The Old Seawitch would not be a long hike. Luckily, Mr. Habbershack hadn't misled us all.

By now the sky had darkened and as soon as we stepped out of the cove you could see the pub sign edged in neon lightbulbs. The sign was atop a large converted old house, and it was the only restaurant on the street. Bait and tackle shops, a marine dealer, and a small store called Neptune's Fishing Nets encased The Old Seawitch.

As we walked in, I was hit with the smell of smoke and saltwater grime from the local sailors who were unwinding from a long and arduous day. Occasionally a waft of fried fish or seasoned corn and potatoes strolled past on a server's platter. The large open room was dimly light and hazy from the pipes and cigarettes.

Local patrons were glancing over their shoulders at our young female performers, their faces softening at the sight of them. They nodded politely.

Several men in our troupe went straight for the bartender. I noticed Mr. Habbershack was sitting at the bar too, amongst a few other men. They had suspicious looks on their faces and kept their heads together in deep discussion.

The host sat Alex and I in a back corner booth near the bar. Since it was on our own dime, we ordered modestly.

"Ugh, I hate cigarette smoke," I whispered to myself.

"Rock and roll, man," said Alex.

"*Pffft*. How'd it go today, superstar?"

"Good. Mainly setting up the coaster."

"Yeah, I saw a little of that. Looks impressive."

"It should be. As long as I don't fall out of the harness."

"Please don't." I laughed off the comment, but I was always scared of the possibility of Alex falling; even if it was a bit hypocritical considering my own routines. Being completely upside down, he would crash on his skull head-first.

"Ol Habby looks engrossed. Wonder if he's plotting our demise since he seems to dislike this Mr. Hagan character so much," Alex said, glancing at the bar. Mr. Habbershack was animatedly bobbing his head and raising his hands as he spoke.

"Probably doesn't care for the circus freaks invading his watering hole."

"I'm going to go order a drink and eavesdrop," said Alex, smirking and bouncing his eyebrows.

I sat back in the booth and looked around at the decor, which wasn't as alluring as the cove's. The men from our troupe at the bar had downed their first drink by now and were consequently talking louder and laughing more often than when we first arrived. I watched one of them, a juggler, slap Alex on the back and praise him for what a cool act he had. However, his buddy, a fire eater, turned away from them while sipping a beer and rolling his eyes.

Alex was gracious to the juggler and then lingered at the bar. Propping himself up at the bar section nearest Mr. Habbershack's group, trying to look inconspicuous but getting closer to earshot. He hung there awhile, swirling the likely vodka in a glass and sipping it more slowly than usual. When he returned he had a funny look on his face.

"Sooo?" I asked.

"I couldn't hear much. Said something like, 'That jackass got one,' and someone's in cahoots with someone else. Something about a deal. I don't know they were muffled."

"Hmmm, got one what?" I thought aloud.

I was staring at the table thinking when I heard Ava's voice. She and Shay had just walked in and were joining some of the men at the bar. The men looked as awkward as baby giraffes as Ava flirted with them. And by the looks of it, she knew what she was doing. I had to give it to her, some girls have just got it.

"Want me to invite the girls over?" Alex asked.

"Nah, they'll find us I'm sure. Maybe they'll overhear something too."

Our food arrived and Alex was more occupied. I noticed Shay was looking bored watching Ava and the boys, and she insidiously edged toward the side of the bar. Though she pretended to be enthralled with all the nearby conversations, I thought she may be eavesdropping too. Maybe even intermittently lip reading. After a while, we made eye contact. I waved a hand at her. She touched Ava's arm to let her know she was excusing herself from the third wheeled conversation, and I scooted further in the booth to let her sit by me.

"So. I know you weren't listening to Ava. What did you hear?" I asked her as she settled in.

"It was very insightful, actually," she answered, pleased with herself.

"Go on," said Alex, "I've already had my shift, and all I got was something about somebody getting something and somebody making a deal."

"Oh, well, I didn't hear anything about that. And both of you are sure to dispute everything I'm about to say." Shay eyed both of us.

"We can hold it in." I gave her a doe eyed look of innocence.

"Okay then," Shay took a breath, "I heard that the merpeople are collecting the algae for Mr. Hagan's businesses in exchange for safety. And that Mr. Hagan is blackmailing them to comply since his father, a sailor, was murdered by one of the merpeople. And that he threatens to notify and assist the marine biologist in catching and experimenting on them if they were to stop aiding him. How's that?"

Alex and I just looked at her with braindead stares for a minute, though she seemed unfazed.

"You're yanking our chain," Alex said.

"Nope."

"How in the world could you have possibly heard all that?" he asked.

"Yeah," I pushed, "I watched you and them. They weren't speaking enough to get all of that."

"Let's just say I have a gift," Shay replied.

"What kind of gift?" I pressed, gawking at her. "Wait a minute. You know everything. About the Mandevilles. About the crew. The other day—it was like you could see what I was thinking."

Shay stared at her lap, "I figured you would find out sooner or later since we spend so much time together. And since I don't see you getting kicked out anytime soon."

"You're like... clairvoyant?"

"No no no," she lowered her voice, "I can't see the future. I'm a mind reader. I can hear thoughts," Shay replied, looking up hesitantly to see if we would freak out.

After a minute of bewilderment, Alex broke the silence, "This is awesome. We can find out anything!"

"Who all knows?" I asked.

"Just my close friends. Ava. A few aerial partners. I'd prefer if you don't share it."

"No, of course not," Alex and I both shook our heads. "Do the Mandevilles know?" I asked.

"Yes. And they don't love that I can infiltrate their thoughts. So they often avoid being very close to me. I have to be in close proximity to a person to hear what they're thinking."

"What am I thinking of now?" Alex asked.

"Shrimp kabobs."

"And now?" Alex's eyes were growing wider.

"Hot fudge sundae."

There was another pause.

"That Janie has something in her teeth."

"What!?" I covered my mouth quickly.

"This is so awesome!" Alex was giddy.

Shay sat up very straight and crossed her arms on the table, "I have some rules. I try not to tell any thoughts that would hurt other people. Especially the people I care about. And if you ask me, I reserve the right to refuse enlightening you with answers. I prefer you speak to me rather than assuming there's no need since I can read your mind. I like to be treated normally, like everyone else."

"Got it," I replied slowly, and then we all got quiet again.

"Don't make this awkward. Carry on as usual," said Shay frustratedly.

"Right. Yeah, okay. So these men really believe in merpeople?"

"I daresay you'll be believers soon enough," said Shay.

We eyed her suspiciously. What did she know? Such a beautiful girl with such an extraordinary gift. Not to mention a very polished aerialist, expert in so many apparatuses and styles. No wonder she had some sway with the Mandevilles.

"Can I ask you another question?" I asked.

"Sure."

"Did you have to learn mind reading or were you just born with it?"

Shay sighed and relaxed into the booth, "When I was little, before I could talk, my mother says I cried and cried all the time. There were so many voices nearby, in and out, because in Blue Smoke Bog we lived in an old house with four other families. All with their own set of issues, as every family faces. One couple fought all the time, so their thoughts were always angry and feverish in tone. Startling to a small child. Another family had children who weren't impressed with sharing attention in the house with a new baby. Anyway, when I began to talk my mother sort of figured it out. Apparently the gift runs in our family, though it skips generations. My great grandmother had told my mother about it when she was a little girl, captivating her with readings." Shay paused in thought.

"Blue Smoke Bog. That's where you're from, right?" I asked.

"Well, I was born there. I learned how to harness my gift there. It's an odd and unique sort of place. In the area where we lived, there was a history of Vodun people.

Some from my family line, though very distant, practiced voodoo. My great grandmother strayed away from it, chalked her abilities up to a gift to be used for the power of good. She was very aged when I became old enough to understand and talk about my ability. She guided me in how to channel my focus, so I could function normally and be at peace. But she died after just a few months of mentoring me. The rest I've figured out on my own. And as soon as she passed, we left Blue Smoke Bog. I was six years-old."

"And eventually you joined Carlyle's Carnival of Wonders?" I asked.

"Yes, as an aerialist only."

"And that's where you first met Reginald Mandeville."

"Yes."

"So you know the entire story of the Mandevilles. From the very start. What really went down when Carlyle ended up dead and Reginald took over," I said.

"That is a story for another day. You and I both need to call it a night soon."

It was nearing nine o'clock. She had a good point. We would have to ferry over early in the morning and be at the fairgrounds all day. It was sure to be a long one.

"I guess you're right," I said to Shay, looking around the smoky room. Most of the wooden lacquered booths were empty now. Ava must have been escorted back because she was no longer there, filling the air with giggles. People were winding down and dwindling out.

The bartender served a last call beer to a tired stranger on a stool and began wiping down the bar.

"Hey, Zeke and Daniel never made it. Guess I should order something to go for them," said Alex.

"You better do it fast. It's closing time."

Alex walked up to the waitress who was idling around slowly cleaning tables until quitting time.

I looked at Shay, "I promise I won't tell anyone. I'm glad you felt comfortable sharing that with me. And I'll try not to bug you with questions."

"You're a good person, Janie. I trust you." Shay winked at me and patted my knee as she got up from the booth.

As she walked out the door of The Old Seawitch, I caught the stranger at the bar eyeing her up and down. I couldn't imagine what all she heard. Warranted and unwarranted. She had to be strong to stomach it all. Sure you could find out things, use the gift to your advantage. But you also heard the other side of it. People's true motives, people conniving ways to advance by using you, people thinking you are beneath them. My heart ached for her at the thought of it.

Alex came back with a carry-out bag, and we headed out of the pub. We were both quiet walking home, lost in thought. When we got to the hallway cross roads of the cove, Zeke was walking back towards his room from the very end of the hall. Alex shook the bag at him as he neared.

"Too good for The Old Seawitch or you just didn't want to eat tonight?" he teased.

"Nooo," Zeke smiled, closing his eyes and wiggling his chin back and forth. "I lost track of time. I wanted to make sure Tombo was inconspicuously set up in our room."

"How did you manage to bring Tombo back to the cove?" I asked with an impressed tone.

"I made my case to Anthony. And he was actually quite nice about it. Said he would clear it up with the Mandevilles. So hopefully he's done that by now or they don't notice."

"Anthony okayed it? Well that's great," I replied.

"Yeah, maybe you can stop moping around now," Alex ragged.

"I feel much better already. I've never been separated from Tombo like that. I worried myself sick. Now I can breathe again."

"What were you doing down the hallway," Alex asked.

"Oh, Anthony's room is at the end. I just wanted to thank him again."

"In his room?" I raised my eyebrows.

"Relax, I was in there for less than two minutes. And keep it down, I don't want everyone in the troupe to hear about it." Zeke glanced up and down the hallways.

"He rooms alone?"

"Evidently."

"Anything interesting in his lodging?"

"Just lots of notebooks. Some sketches. Apparently he can draw too."

"So what, he's like a circus designer?" Alex asked sarcastically.

"Watch it, mister. If anyone needs the services of a designer, it's you."

"Alright, alright," said Alex, handing the food to Zeke. "I'll drop it. You better eat up though. I paid good money for that. Half is Daniel's," he turned to me, "Goodnight, Janie."

"Night, guys!"

I walked down the quiet hall to my room. Without the distraction of the boys and the bar and the information Shay just dropped on me, it didn't take very long for me to realize how close I was to my first circus performance. A performance in which the Mandevilles would be extra critical, since they had something to gain from building a relationship with Mr. Hagan.

Chapter 12

The Side Show Addition

The morning arrived and brought a strikingly aesthetic day. The sun was out early and the sky was clear with a few big, puffy, cotton balls of clouds carefully placed in the troposphere.

As we rode the ferry boat to the fairgrounds, the sea was lit up and showing off a beautiful shade of turquoise. The sun's rays on my skin brought a welcome serving of energy. Even if the price of it was sweat, which made me feel sticky in my practice leggings. Nevertheless, I was thankful for the heat and tried to relax as we floated across the water.

Since it was warmer, the trek down the dock of the marina and through the path along the saw palmettos was like a hike through a small jungle. I didn't mind it, but I could see that Ava was miffed by the humidity mother nature had provided us. She emitted sounds of muffled huffs as she carried her hoops across her shoulder, wiping her brow with the back of her hand, and smoothing out her pony tail every yard or so.

Once inside the fairground building, the troupe slowed to a halt in front of the Mandevilles. Reginald looked particularly upbeat this morning. He rocked back and forth on his heels, his hands held behind his back, and smiling as we all drew near. Caroline, on the other hand, did not reflect his mood. She clasped her hands in front of her lightly and glanced around the room, blank faced.

"Settle in, kids," Reg called out across the room. "All right, I informed you all there would be a new side show." He snapped and nodded at Anthony, who stood by the door of the side entrance.

Anthony walked out the door for a minute and then reappeared with two men rolling a large circus wagon through the entry. They pushed it to a stop just about four yards away from us.

The ornately designed wagon reminded me of a Romani gypsy vardo. Lacquered in emerald green with silver filigree encasing the cage bars. Elaborately carved wooden hub caps, painted silver to match the filigree, hid the substantially sized wheel spokes.

Behind the iron cage bars appeared to be a large case concealed by purple crushed velvet fabric. Intermittently between the breaths of Reginald's monologue, I thought I heard sloshing. And the smell of the marina dock had somehow returned.

As Reg broke out into speech, Anthony looked apprehensive and stood as far away from the wagon as could be unnoticed that it was intentional. And Caroline seemed to follow suit.

"Ladies and gentleman, you are about to witness something that will put our circus over the top. It will astound not only the audience, but the locals of Merdwick and Mr. Hagan himself. Not only that, but also raise our ticket sales in the shows to come."

The performers were on their guard, glancing between the Mandevilles and the wagon repetitively.

Reg continued, "Now. Yesterday I instructed you all not to make a fuss or disclose any information about this side show to anyone. The last thing I need is to start a riot or revolt of the locals. And as to how I've acquired it is none of your business."

Hearing this, I glanced at Shay as inconspicuously as possible. She looked strained. She must have been too far away to hear anything.

Reg turned, beaming at Caroline, "Darling, would you do the honors," he said, extending a black leather gloved hand toward the cage. She smiled at him, though it looked like she was communicating something to him through her eyes. A solid stare that speaks. He encouraged her onward with a gentle push on her lower back. The two men, who had rolled the cage inside, opened the side doors of the wagon and stepped back.

She approached in impressively graceful trepidation. She slowly and lightly rolled each finger onto the fabric atop the case and scrunched it into her palm. A stiff pause, an inhale. You could have heard a pin drop in that echoing high ceiling building, and the pause felt twenty minutes long. Though I knew in Caroline's haste it could have only lasted for two or three seconds.

She pulled and took four sweeping steps back with the fabric, as if it was all just part of a dance routine. There were startled steps in all directions from the performers. Gasps and hands rising up towards chests and mouths.

The pull of the fabric revealed a plexiglass case filled with water and copious strands of floating seaweed. Within the dancing swirls of seaweed, a great fishlike creature was rolling towards our side of the cage to face us.

Upon first glimpse, it was a tan beige color, speckled with black spots, and very skinny and long. As it turned through the water, a slender arm emerged from the grass. The thing's chest was slowly turning from supine to side lying.

Behind the seaweed, in one corner of the case, was a silhouette of what could only be a head. A webbed hand brushed the grass down the length of the fishtail, toward the opposite end of the tank, and unveiled it.

Before our troupe, within the glass and water, a face was now gaping at us. Scrutinizing us. Its smooth head peaked into a ridge at the top of its scalp. There were two tiny crevices where nostrils might be, but no ears. Yet these were minor observations. Its eyes were the most striking feature.

The creature had two orbital and bulbous eyes. Three times the size of a human's, considering the size ratio of eyes to face. They stuck out of its head and were a solid sparkly cobalt blue. Dark with no pupils, no way of knowing what exactly they were fixated on. Like snow globes in which the snow never settled.

Chatter rose in the room and Reginald projected his voice over it, "What you have before you is an infamous Merdwick mermaid. Or merperson. I don't know the sex of the thing. What I do know is that it will sway CEO Hagan towards lucrative favor, and that it can be extremely dangerous. Don't even touch the glass."

It was difficult to maintain my composure. I looked at Alex, who was peering at it in disbelief. When I elbowed him nervously, he didn't move his head. Shay appeared disgusted, though I was unsure if it was at the sight of the mermaid or at the Mandevilles for its capture. Ava and Daniel looked scared. Zeke baffled. The other side show acts were a mixture of all the above.

Caroline must have noted a rise in the overall adrenaline of the troupe because she spoke up. "Troupe, this will be an exhibition piece only. Anthony will handle its transport and maintenance. Now, we have a long day and a long night ahead of us. So you are to divvy up and begin practice promptly after breakfast."

Anthony placed the velvet covering over the glass and instructed the men to roll the wagon back out of the building. The Mandevilles led the way into the adjoining room for breakfast, Reginald still visibly excited about his latest acquisition. He wrapped an arm around Caroline and started animatedly talking to her as they went; Anthony trailing behind them.

The circus crew took a few minutes to settle before making their way to breakfast.

"I told you. Always acquiring unique acts," said Zeke as we began walking.

There was some brouhaha during breakfast over the mermaid for the first fifteen minutes or so. But this cast of characters was used to strange and wearisome components of the circus coming in or getting kicked off. As long as they weren't made to mess with it, care for it or interact with it, they were fine. It was the rookies like Alex and myself that were unsettled by it most. Particularly because we were so skeptical of its existence in the first place.

Alex decided that maybe he was wrong. Maybe there were merpeople in the sea near Merdwick. Feral creatures, like animals, unsophisticated. However, he was not quick to jump on the idea that they were supporting the algae business with labor due to being blackmailed.

But I was growing more and more trusting of Shay. She had only heard thoughts—and sometimes thoughts are not true—but to me, it seemed to make sense that there had to be some merit to it. Why else would Reginald bother with catching one? If Mr. Hagan did hate merpeople, he'd be thrilled to see one exploited. And Reg was determined to become a shareholder.

Practice was as usual, though with additional sweat since it was a warm day and the sun was beaming in through the skylight windows. Shay and I warmed up in the adjacent breakfast room; since the roustabouts were setting up the layout of the grand room, where the show would be performed.

Midday, we took a break and checked on the progress. The main room was coming around and it looked like the roustabouts were close to finishing. Since there was seating on all sides of the room, everything had to be thoughtfully orchestrated.

The open floor area held a humongous amount of space, so there was plenty of room to set up for the acts. Green and silver striped canvas swooped and attached to cover the white walls, creating an illusion that it was more of a tent than a building. A roustabout tested all the different colors of lighting.

I was excited and impressed to see Alex's roller coaster track would travel from the north end of the room, up and over the high wire, and across to the south end. There were two steel tracks that his drum set platform was attached between. Once enough clearance was gained, the platform itself would rotate forwards or backwards three hundred and sixty degrees. Everyone in the room would have a good view. I could just imagine his elation and eagerness to try it out.

Under the coaster track, near the north side, was a large cage for the big cat tamer. In the middle of the room was a section with foot tall curved barriers where the horse whisperers, and Daniel and Eloise, would perform within a defined space. Other acts such as Reginald's sword swallowing and Caroline's contortions would take place in the center. On the south end of the room, various platforms were erected for balancing acts and jugglers. I assumed the clowns would run amuck. And the side show acts were set up in green striped tents near the entrances outside, to entertain folks as they were coming in or leaving.

Shay and I would perform smack dab in the center of the room. The cube was rigged adjacent to the high wire. It would be lowered for us to climb onto and then rise fifty feet in the air; which was high for me. My palms began to sweat as I looked at it.

"It's exactly the same routine, same transitions, same poses. Whether you are five or fifty feet from the ground. You're ready," Shay said, wrapping an arm around my shoulders.

"I know. It'll be fine. I'm fine. It's going to be great," I said in response, but more to myself than to Shay. "The place looks amazing."

"It does. I'm not wild about the green and silver, but I guess it matches the ambience of a sea town. Did you notice where they're putting the king of Merdwick?" Shay pointed toward a Victorian style dark wood and red velvet couch.

"VIP?"

"For Mr. Hagan, of course," Shay said in a mocking proper voice of a servant to the monarchy.

"Geez. No pressure, huh?" I said sarcastically.

"Eh, it doesn't really matter. You've gotta have fun with it to get by around here."

"Yeah, but my head is still on the Mandevilles' chopping block."

Shay waved that comment off, "Let's go try it out now. Front and center. That way it's not you're first time when we do the show tonight."

I followed her to the cube reluctantly. The tight roper was doing the same, trying out the wire high above us. And about that time, Alex walked in to practice on the actual platform to get a feel for it. I waved at him and lifted my hands by my shoulders, scanning the track with my eyes to convey my amazement. He opened his eyes very wide and grinned like a little kid at Christmas.

Shay had a roustabout lower and secure the cube. We got into position on each side of it, holding onto the cold steel, and walking around in a circle to give it a spin. On count we inverted, and then positioned ourselves seated on top of a bar, kicking our feet slowly and gracefully back and forth with pointed toes.

"Could you hoist us up a little, Henry?" Shay called out to the roustabout.

Steadily we rose to twenty feet, thirty feet, forty feet. We stopped at fifty feet high, slowly spinning and continuing kicks from our perch.

"See, same thing," said Shay.

"If I don't look down."

"Focus on the movements. And on the music tonight. The music always helps me."

I followed Shay's lead to get back on count, and we went through our entire routine. After the first two minutes, I got more comfortable and stopped looking around the room so much. By four minutes, I was focused on hitting poses. And near the end of our routine, I was actually having fun.

"Alright, Henry. Can you bring us back down?" Shay called.

"Nooope," a voice rang back.

Shay laughed and swung her dark wavy hair back. She was as comfortable and at home up in the air as I had ever seen her. Away from the noise and voices and inner dialogues of people's minds.

"Fine, I guess I'll let you down," Henry said sarcastically.

We descended and continued the routine by gracefully hanging from a bar until our feet pressed against the floor. We strode in sweeping steps across the floor like ballerinas and lifted our arms up to the imaginary audience. A grand ta-da. Alex began clapping loudly from his platform. We curtsey to him playfully.

"I told you. You're ready," said Shay.

"Maybe," I breathed, "In leggings and a tank top. But I just realized, I have no idea what I'll be wearing or have on top of my head up there."

"Anthony is procuring all costumes. Ava heard that they are all ocean themed. I can't wait to see them," said Shay. "We go to dressing and makeup an hour and a half before the show."

We talked through the routine once more, in the adjoining room, and spent the late afternoon doing yoga and stretching the stiffest muscles. I thought waiting on show time would be agonizing, but it quickly became time to get costumed and ready.

The dressing room housed a hustle and bustle that I had only seen in movies. It was like being backstage at a runway show. Thankfully, it was unintegrated by the male performers because women were briskly traversing the room, hastily changing into costumes. Modesty was minimal. I was relieved that Shay led our navigation through the chaos to the garment rack.

Hanging there was a costume within a clear plastic suit cover that had a large tag which read my name on it. It was a stunning leotard covered in teal and emerald green sequins. Long mesh skin colored sleeves had pearl beads sewed sporadically into them. Around the lower waist was a short beaded skirt of the same colors and pearls. And in a small bag attached to the hook of the hanger was a clam shell hair clip that was painted an iridescent purple. It had a tiny starfish and several pearls encrusted on it.

Shay's costume matched my own. But some other ladies had costumes that emphasized characteristics of jellyfish, starfish, or octopi.

I took my costume to a corner and tried to change as discreetly as possible. After I had neatly folded and stowed away my practice clothes, Shay sculpted my hair into a tight side bun and slicked back the stray, fuzzy hairs with some gel. Once the hair clip was applied, we went to wait on makeup.

There were quite a few women for one makeup artist to conquer, but this lady was a pro. She spent about five minutes on each face. And by the time she was done, they had evolved from a natural human face to a masterful work of art. From a humble caterpillar to a psychedelic butterfly. I wondered what in the world I might be transformed into.

Graciously, Shay stepped up to her vanity first. From where I stood, I could only see the back of Shay's head, her shoulders relaxed and low. The makeup artist's arms and gangly elbows were flying.

Brushes were dabbing into small containers and swishing back and forth across the canvas of Shay's face. Flecks of opalescent plastic and shimmering glitter tapped out of tubes. The makeup artist stood back and leaned her head to one side, examining the progress. Then she dove back in, strategically placing prismatic sequins along Shay's temples.

Her furious hands finally slowed, and I was intrigued, imagining what the final product might look like in my head. The makeup artist spun Shay around in the chair to excuse her and revealed an alluring showpiece that was mermaid inspired. She had created an illusion of fish scales tastefully contouring Shay's cheekbones and forehead.

Shay winked at me as the artist hastily beckoned me forward. As I stood in front of the chair, the lady pushed my shoulders down to expedite the process of getting seated. I figured I shouldn't bother with any chit chat so I just closed my eyes.

The artist swashed various textures across my face. Cold and sticky creams, brushes of soft powder, dabs of something like glue. She poked me with her finger nails as she applied facial sequins. And then, in a flash, she laconically spat, "Finished." I caught a quick glimpse in her mirror before she shoved me aside and beckoned forth the next performer.

"We match," said Shay, "Come, there's a mirror over here."

I cautiously followed her, but when I looked in the mirror, I was pleasantly surprised to find that I did match Shay. I imagined two mermaids flipping around an underwater shipwreck's boom, complimenting and reflecting each other's movements in unison. That would be Shay and I. Only in the air across metal, and with posing legs instead of tails.

"We look magical," I breathed.

"And that we are, darling," said Shay in a mock Victorian English accent.

We were about thirty minutes away from show time. I couldn't help but investigate whether or not an actual crowd was coming in. I snuck out the dressing room and around to one entrance. Through the window, I could see the courtyard where the side shows were performing. Sure enough, there was a gathering of folks in pairs and families, milling about the side show tents outside and awaiting entry.

I could see Master Kai, the strong man, shoulder pressing a great barbell with giant metal spheres two feet in diameter on each side. Big Bertha hiked a heavy knee up and propped her foot on a stool. She pushed back her skirt to reveal a leg almost as thick as Eloise's. Families were spectating and gasping in surprise.

Inside a tent with its entry way tied open, I caught glimpses of the snake charmer between people walking by. She was sitting cross-legged on a colorful Indian floor cushion, honking and blowing on a pungi. A cobra bobbed around in front of her. Children were being tugged backwards and away at the collars of their shirts by their wary mothers.

Where was the merperson? I searched across the growing crowd until my eyes met the circus wagon, distantly placed from the throngs of people. The velvet fabric was still draped over the case and veiled the creature. Roustabouts rolled the wagon behind the building as I watched, and I wondered where it would make its stop. Why didn't they leave it outside?

The smell of popcorn perfumed the air, and the noise of people getting seated began to rise in volume as we all waited. Caroline was making rounds to each room of performers. She instructed us to be attentive to our cues to transition in and out of the grand room.

Chapter 13

I Present To You...

By six thirty, there was a growing roar beckoning the show to begin. Reginald would be in his private dressing room finishing the final touches to his wardrobe. A velvet coat of dark crimson with gold buttons, the coattails of which hung just a foot above the ground. Black leather boots that came up just below the knee. And finally, a large black top hat with a royal blue ribbon wrapping around the band. I could just imagine him applying wax and curling the ends of his mustache, admiring his own reflection in the mirror before him. Grinning that cunning grin, like he knows something the rest of us don't. Like he had something none of us could ever have.

The lights spun across the room, over the faces of men, women, and children sitting in the dark, eager for what their eyes may behold next. Flashes of pink, green, and yellow whizzed around and landed on the wide-eyed wonder of old and young. Whispers and gasps dispersed within the building that had now transformed into an arena of wonders.

The calliope sounded, tooting out loud jolly notes, a mix between a church organ and a train whistle. Trumpets, trombones, and tubas began to honk as well.

The clowns spread in from the side entrances and wandered throughout the rows in the crowd. They waved and shook the hands of children. To get a laugh, they pulled coins from ears or pretended to be tripped by the corresponding parents. Laughter mixed with the sounds of instruments at the time of the grand opening.

The show began with a trail of animals paraded through the center ring. In succession were the domestic animals, the horses, and our beloved Eloise. The big cats filtered into their giant cage somewhere in between. The audience had a hard time keeping their eyes on any one aspect of the introduction. There was so much going on. So much sound and color.

And naturally, Reginald entered cane in hand as a grand spot light followed him like a lap dog and slowed to a stop on a platform at the center of the ring. His voice rang out, crashing and bouncing off walls, widening the eyes of the spectators.

"For the benefit of Mr. Hagan, ladies and gentlemen, I present to you a show second to none. A show that remains the most spectacular and peculiar, the most amazing and transcendent. A show so magnificent that it's hard for the human psyche to believe. Ladies and gentlemen, I present to you The Mandevilles' Marvelous Marvels!"

As he finished his intro, he executed a grandiose spin. With his arm extended gracefully, he bowed to Mr. Hagan, who was seated front and center on a luxurious throne of a chair. Big enough that his wife could sit beside him. Mr. Hagan clapped, lifting his hands up and toward Reginald in acknowledgement. His appearance reminded me of a fat cat in a skyscraper. I could imagine him wearing a pinstriped suit and kicked back in a chair counting money, his bald crown and greased down hair rimming the lower half of his head as he thumbed bills.

Back in the adjoining rooms I could feel the growing lump in my throat, and the hairs on my neck and arms rose. I mentally told myself to relax my shoulders, and jumped and jostled about to keep my blood from mottling up and paralyzing me. Everyone else looked very at ease, all pros who had been in this game for a while now. I wondered how Alex was feeling, but he wasn't anywhere in sight, and I dared not leave Shay's side. She was like my security blanket at this point.

The show began with the jugglers, followed by Ava's hula hoop routine. Three jugglers leisurely tossed their items. Bottles, bowling pins, and plastic balls that resembled a croquet set were rotating fluidly through the air in a magnificent ring that almost reached the high wire.

After about five minutes, they parted the pathway to the center ring and Ava bounced in. I didn't think her smile could grow any wider, but tonight it was not only enormous but genuine.

She wore a hot pink sequin bodysuit, the bodice dazzling like a million little pink mirrors. Like a human disco ball. The sequins floated away from her middle in swirls like reef coral, down her legs and arms. She donned a small set of white feathers on top of her head. They couldn't be very large for fear they would get pulled out during her hoop routine. Her blonde hair, curled and pinned in rings all around her scalp, was a throwback to the nineteen twenties.

She wore it all very well. All the young men in the audience were gawking as her electric blue eyes scanned the room, winking as she started to hoop.

Ava began hula hooping a single hoop all the way from her calves to her neck. She stuck an arm through and spun the hoop around her wrist. From there she began several illusions, flipping the hoop behind her waist and head, rolling it across the back of her shoulders. She manipulated it back around her waist and added two more hoops. They orbited her neck, waist, and calves in perfect sections.

An assistant stepped out to aid her and tossed a hoop toward her extended hand, which she caught and continued to rotate before placing it over her head. She rotated the other hoops down her body to make room for it.

Ever the character—after about three additional hoops had been tossed to her, she shot the audience a faux gasp of shock and aggravation which elicited a response from everyone in the room. Women and children giggled, men began drooling. After a moment, she let the hoops slowly travel to the floor.

The final trick of Ava's act was a hoop routine from atop her walking globe. After flipping onto the globe, she transitioned to a graceful perch and hooped the giant rings on her feet. From there she moved into a standing position and rolled the walking globe across the center stage floor as her assistant continued to throw her more rings. Eventually, she had three rotating around her body, as she spun two others cyclically around each hand.

She tossed them back to the assistant one by one, and then executed a perfect handstand on top of the globe before flipping down to the center of the stage. She struck a pose that would make a gymnast's coach proud, and the audience bellowed praise.

As she strode out of the ring, the next set of performers pranced in. Lions and Tigers were made to roll across the floor or stand on their hind legs. The horse whisperer guided beautiful mares to stride in alternating patterns that were accentuated by the contrast of the colors of their coats. Fire eaters blew massive flames toward the ceiling like angry dragons.

On the high wire, the lead tight roper donned a magnificent costume inspired by sea anemone, curtesy of Anthony of course. To aid in balance, she held a large umbrella crafted to look like a jelly fish. Its tentacles made of a light and flowing translucent material that swayed as she carefully stepped along the wire.

Daniel and Eloise made their Merdwick debut next. Daniel wore a gold patterned suit with a sequin cummerbund, a white ruffle around his neck, and a red bowler hat atop his head. His eyes bright behind the lenses of his glasses. Eloise was cloaked in a blanket and headdress that complimented Daniel's costume.

Daniel's smile was wider than Ava's. He patted Eloise lovingly on her side and led her around the ring for viewing before guiding her to the platform and instructing her to sit on it, just as a human would sit on a stool. The crowd laughed and pointed. Next, she balanced upside down on her two front legs and trunk; a giant tripod. Then she reared up on her hind legs as if she were a stallion in a western movie.

As Eloise stepped down from the platform, trunk curled and shaking her head from side to side while the crowd enlivened, Ava reappeared in the center ring with a rainbow lighted hoop spinning across her waist. Daniel clapped and fanned his hands toward her to welcome her to the ring as the crowd continued to cheer.

Ava translated the hoop up and over her neck and around her wrist; her arm straight up in the air. Eloise stuck her trunk through its center and pulled it up off of Ava's hand, continuing to spin it as she raised up on her hind legs once more.

Mr. Hagan raised and clapped his hands as he chuckled. The charming pachyderm continued hooping the lighted ring as she exited.

When Eloise's swishing tail was out of sight, the ambience of the room transformed. The lights were dimmed, and a spotlight fixated on the center of the ring. A clown assisted by placing a platform coated in sparkling black glitter in the lighted area.

The audience quieted, suspicious of the dramatic contrast from loud colors and lights to dark silence. Slowly, an accordion played. The dynamics of the melody rising and falling in an ominous manner.

Caroline Mandeville stepped in from the shadows. She wore a skin tight leotard with red and black patterns of sea urchins scattered flatteringly across the otherwise nude colored suit. I had never seen her in a costume, and it took me awhile to grasp the fact that she would do anything other than float around our troupe in garb as elegant as a royal gown.

Standing before the platform, she flexed her spine and thrust her arms forward making her body into a giant C. She took hold of the far edge of the stand with her hands, set her chest on top of it, and extended her spine in the opposite direction until her hindquarters hovered over her head; her legs scissored at the knee in pose. After holding for several seconds, she landed her feet in front of her head. She slid her torso backwards, out from under her legs, until she was in a hands free backbend. From there she unraveled herself back to a regular standing position.

Hinged at the hips, she crossed her arms before placing her hands lightly on the tops of her feet, and then twisted her torso completely around to face the crowd.

She lifted a hand and curled each finger in a flirtatious wave at the crowd.

Next, she transitioned into the splits. The audience gasped, though Caroline was totally at ease. From the splits she rolled her torso backwards until her weight was on her stomach, so that she could pull one leg forward and split again; her legs in the air rather than on the ground.

At this time, there was another entry to the ring. Reginald Mandeville strode in and slung his arms towards his wife as he took a position on the ground beside her platform and the spot light expanded. The audience clapped heartily.

Caroline transitioned to a standing bow pose, and Reginald placed his top hat upon her head as she held her position. From there Caroline continued a number of complex contortions as an assistant brought Reginald a modest sized dagger, thin in the blade. He licked up and down the dagger ceremoniously, rested the tip on his tongue, then tilted his head back and slowly lowered the blade down his throat.

Reg extended his arms and stepped around three hundred and sixty degrees, giving spectators a view of each angle. Gasps and grimaces resounded. Whispers of shock between family members reverberated throughout the room amongst clapping hands. Reg pulled the dagger from his throat and waved it at the audience. Next, a larger blade and a car axle. Following those, he swallowed a glowing saber as roustabouts dimmed the lights for added effect.

Finally, the assistant presented him with a rather large sword. Thick bladed with shining silver metal extending to twenty-four inches in length. The hilt encrusted with gemstones and gilded with gold.

In the same manner, though dragging it out to increase suspense, Reg lifted the sword and slid it down his throat. Again he rotated his body for the crowds viewing. And as he did so, Caroline assumed a handstand position and folded herself in a back bend; to where her left leg extended directly in front of her head and her right leg shot straight up toward the ceiling. She then shifted her weight to balance in this position on one arm. As she held the pose, Reginald turned to face her and bent forward at the hips so he could meet her eye line, his body in a ninety-degree angle.

With her free hand, Caroline slowly reached forward and grasped the hilt of the blade. In what seemed an agonizingly slow fashion, she pulled it. Its tip leaving the area near Reginald's lower esophageal sphincter, beside his thumping heart, adjacent his jugular vein, and out of his great mustache bordered mouth.

The crowd shrieked in delight, standing and clapping like their lives depended on it. Music transitioned from slow and brooding to booms of triumph.

A few droplets of sweat sat perched on Reginald's brow as Caroline extended the sword for him to take from her. She gracefully rolled out of the pose and flipped down from the platform next to him. The two of them wrapped an arm around each other's waist and bowed to a perseveringly encouraging crowd. They looked each other in the eyes, grins on their faces, and Reginald laid a big kiss onto Caroline's mouth. Her eyelashes fluttering as he pulled away and their grins reappearing. Mr. Hagan and his wife stood, clapping and shouting "bravo!"

"An intermission will commence at this time and last for fifteen minutes. Please enjoy the concessions, and you wouldn't want to go home without a Mr. or Mrs. Mandeville doll. That's right! A Mrs. Mandeville doll can bend at all angles! And a Mr. Mandeville doll of course swallows a variety of included swords! Kids, these are sure to make your friends jealous!" Anthony's voice rang throughout the arena.

"They would have their own dolls," I thought to myself. And I wasn't surprised to see that children were pulling their parents by the sleeves and begging them to buy a toy made in the likeness of the infamous ring leader and his bendy bride. Honestly, if I had been a little girl, I would have asked my daddy for both, so I could re-enact the act I had just been mesmerized by at home.

"We're up next. First act after the intermission," said Shay.

My stomach dropped to my feet and my palms started to sweat. Nervous bladder hit, which pushed my anxiety higher.

Shay smoothed her face in mocking glee, like those ads of a mother pushing a vacuum across her living room floor in the fifties. A sarcastic way of assuaging my nerves. And I knew she had read my mind because the next words out of her mouth were, "Let me show you to the restrooms."

"I've never performed that high in front of that many people. I don't know about this," I said.

"Well, you have to now. So you better know," Shay retorted matter-of-factly. "This is a duo routine. It won't work without you. No one else knows it. And you can't leave me out there to do it all myself."

I took some deep breaths and jumped up and down a couple times before we exited the restroom. "Okay. Alright. It's just like practice, but with people. I can do this," I started to mantra to myself.

"That's the spirit," said Shay as we walked out and ran smack into Reginald. He was toweling off his brow and had temporarily doffed his jacket to cool down. He was more built and muscular than I had realized, and unfortunately this made him a bit more intimidating than he already was.

"Ladies," he nodded, "Let's see you two follow that routine!" He chuckled for a minute. "Oh, look at your faces. I'm kidding, I'm kidding. Well, I know Shay can handle it, but now comes the time to see if you can keep up with the big boys," he said as he slapped the back of my shoulder hard enough to cause me to stumble forward. "Whoa, is this one already dizzy? You better get it together, girl." The chuckles morphed into guffaws.

"We were just making our way to side stage. You know, if there's no black marketed creatures blocking entry," Shay spoke as smoothly as if she was talking about the weather. But my eyes grew in surprise.

Reginald stopped laughing, "Watch yourself, Shay. And I wouldn't be too sure that this girl is worth your trouble in defending."

"Of course, sir," Shay bowed her chin to him, but retained a soft peaceful smile on her face. Reg stomped off.

"Stunning. Literally," was all I could get out.

Shay shrugged a sarcastic look of innocence. "The show must go on," she replied.

Chapter 14

Frights and Delights

We were down to the last three minutes of intermission. The lights flickered inside the arena, letting spectators know to come back to their seats. Families clambered back into their rows and plopped down in chairs.

Shay and I walked out across the center ring under dimmed lights. I tried to keep my face forward, though my eyes darted all around the room, taking in the amount of faces that would have their gaze upon us in just a few moments.

We stopped to tell Henry we were about to assume starting positions, and he lowered the cube as the room grew darker. It was hard to see our spot markers, which didn't ease my nerves, but once we found and stood on them, the melodious notes of our song began to billow throughout the room. It was now or never.

The pink and blue lights slowly raised and brightened to reveal us. We shimmered and gleamed in all our adorned sequins. Shay winked at me.

We each took hold of the bars and began stepping in a circle to catalyst the rotation of the cube. I attempted to plaster a smile on my face, though my lips would not stop quivering. I hoped no one else could tell.

As we continued to step around, Henry raised the cube and we floated up, our feet still synchronized, walking on air. Some in the crowd were already applauding lightly.

We transitioned and hooked one knee on the bottom bar of the cube. From there we held each other's foot down and split our free leg forward. Hanging and back to back with each other, we curved and spun like a pair of horses on a merry-go-round. Next, we moved up to the center of the cube and perched on the bar facing each other, mirroring each other's arm movements. It reminded me of my daydream, where we were mermaids dancing in a shipwreck.

We could now grasp the top bar of the cube. Facing each other, we inverted and executed a split while upside down. From there, a normal upright split across the bars in the center of the cube, then rolled upside down to a star. We extended our arms and smiled at the audience below us.

The crowd was now clearer, less a blur of faces. I could see children pointing with their mouths agape in excitement. That made it all worthwhile to me. To inspire others, and to make them realize that something they thought wasn't possible, could be. That is the romance of the circus. All forms of the arts push the boundaries of human strength and physical limitations. In this way we can transcend our typical capabilities. We can achieve a whimsical level of beauty and power.

To inspire any man, woman, or child by those means was a privilege and honor. The basis of the addiction that each troupe member here now nursed. The essence of what it meant to be a performer.

From the side bars we completed a pull over and hip balance, facing each other and grinning while playfully alternating our legs with pointed toes. Shay and I were having fun now. Despite everything going on around me, I noticed once more just how at home and happy she was up here. I felt happy to have not let her down due to stage fright. The audience was cheering, oohing and awing routinely now. Every pose was getting a reaction.

Our costumes glowed under the dancing lights as our bodies created artful symmetrical postures. Grace like that of an ancient Chinese crane in flight, a great somersaulting manta ray as it feeds in dark ocean waters, a jaguar leaping across jungle branches with ease and poise.

"We've only got a few more poses until we're off scot-free, and this is pretty fun," I thought to myself. The finale was going smoothly and soon we would descend back down to the floor.

We were to stagger our exits. Shay executed a perfect tuck and roll over the bar to achieve a hanging position. She gracefully kicked her legs as she waited for me to perform the same sequence so we could be lowered elegantly feet first to the ground.

I tucked and rolled over the bar just as Shay had done, but as I was coming to a hanging position, the entire cube jolted downward. One of my hands slipped off the bar, and I was hanging by five measly fingers at about forty feet in the air.

I kicked my legs awkwardly to get momentum and propel my other arm back up to the bar, but it took me two tries to achieve this. It all happened so suddenly that I couldn't focus on anything other than getting both hands back on the bar.

Beneath me the audience shrieked, screaming and gasping in momentary horror. No doubt thinking they were about to witness a major accident or even death during what was supposed to be their happy family entertainment. The music played on and I caught a glimpse of Henry hastily letting the cube back down, a dreadful look of abhorred responsibility on his face.

When we finally reached to the ground, we strode forward towards the audience and bowed. The crowd responded with intense cheering, like an injured football player had made it back up to his feet and could walk off the field. I rushed to Shay's side, and we exited the ring.

"Are you okay," Shay asked as soon as we were out of the grand room, her eyes searching my body up and down for injury.

"I'm fine. It was kind of terrifying at the end. But the rest of it I loved," I was breathing heavy but through a grin of successful completion. Even if it was successful because I did not fall to my impending doom.

"Oh good. It didn't ruin you," said Shay, as her face evolved back to normal.

Henry came running into the room looking like his face was melting to the ground in shame. "Girls, I'm so sorry. I'm so, so sorry. I checked the pulley system before. It must have skipped off the track. I'm so sorry."

We were about to give him some encouragement when Reginald came bounding into the room, his face red as a chili pepper. I thought I may have seen steam coming out of his ears. Seeing his angry countenance snapped me back to reality. I recalled how adamantly he demanded our routine be flawless, and I was met with horror at the realization that he may blame me for this.

"What the hell was that?" He spat at the three of us. Henry jumped in, trying to make up for his error.

"I'm so sorry, Mr. Mandeville. I checked the system before. It was an accident. It must've skipped on the track. It won't happen again."

"You're right about that. You're done," Reginald seethed. "And you," he shot at me, "I knew you wouldn't be worth it. That act ended like a writhing fish out of water."

"I had to get back up," I exclaimed. "It wasn't a planned exit!"

Reginald inhaled a deep breath as his eyes zeroed in on me, "Who do you think you are? Don't you ever talk to me like that. I'll have you pitched into these infested waters so fast no amount of awkward struggle will help you back above the surface."

"Reginald! It was an accident," Shay interjected with concentrated attention to his glaring face. "She's shocked. She's not being insolent. There's no need for threats."

"Threats?!"

"Give her one more chance to make it up," came a smooth serene voice from behind us. Caroline approached with a cautious look on her face, trying to problem solve for a dicey situation. "The second show will have no errors and complete elegance, or she's out."

Reginald looked at her in disbelief. He had started to tremble, near the edge of explosion. She placed a soft hand on chest, right over his heart.

"Darling, we have so many other things to think about. Let's not worry about this now. Let her have one more shot. Think of it as your good deed for the day," she smiled at him, but when she turned back to look at us her eyes were unreadable. "We've got three more acts left."

"Last. Chance." Reginald attempted to breathe slow and controlled, though his mustache quivered, as he glared at Shay and I. He turned, placed his top hat back on his wavy head of hair, and headed back to the arena.

Shortly thereafter, we could hear him over the speakers. He laughed to himself and said, "Ladies and gentleman, What do you think of the little stunt we pulled to make sure you were still awake! That's right folks, this circus has many surprises! I'd advise you all to keep your eyes peeled."

Caroline stared at us intently for a few seconds. I saw a very slight turn up one corner of her mouth that seemed like an effort to smile, and then she went about her way. I started breathing again. Holding it together in face-to-face conflict was not my strong suit.

"Is she on our side?" I asked to Shay.

"I wouldn't count on it," she replied in hushed tones.

Reginald stood next to the Hagans, assuring them with lighthearted humor that all was well with the performers, while Zeke and Tombo's act was beginning in the center ring of the arena.

Zeke brought a welcome, cheery, and warm aura to the grand room. He was decked out in a black and white chunky striped button-up under a swarm of red sequins that comprised a vest and bow tie. Tailored slacks and black bowler hat. Tombo was dressed in his red shorts with gold stars and royal blue suspenders. Together they strode out into the ring, Zeke waving as Tombo followed double stride due to his shorter legs.

A clown placed a platform in the center of the ring for Tombo. It must have been specially made because it matched his costume. A round cylinder with red and gold stripes around the middle and a blue star on top; rising about three feet high.

"Good evening, ladies and gentleman! I'm Zeke and this is my brother Tombo," he began just as he had at his audition.

Tombo's jaw dropped, and he shook his head side to side in disbelief. The crowd was already laughing. The motion of Tombo's lips led spectators to believe he was speaking, as a subtle quiver began at Zeke's Adam's apple.

Zeke's persistent smile gleamed in the lighting. Each pair of eyes in the audience began to jump focus back and forth between them. Trying to make sense of what they were seeing.

"Scientist say we share a common ancestor," Zeke continued.

"Well, you don't get to pick your family," Tombo's lips moved as he crossed his hairy arms and turned to the right side of the crowd with a perplexed look on his wrinkled face.

"But you need me. I'm the one who gives you a voice!"

Tombo furrowed his brow and swatted his hands down dismissively. Warm giggles from little children filled the air.

"Alright then. What if I took it away?" Zeke said, putting his hands on his hips.

Tombo's lips flapped, but no sound was heard. He jumped up and down on the platform, slapping his palms on it in a disgruntled and frustrated fashion. The Hagans chuckled in their front-row seat.

"See. You didn't like that now, did you? You need me." Zeke placed a flat palm at the right corner of his mouth like he was telling a secret to the audience, "And he likes me too."

"I do not. I like women," Tombo continued as Zeke's throat twitched, "Bring back sweet Caroline." Tombo grinned and his eyebrows jumped up and down, which elicited guffawing all around.

Zeke mocked surprise and wariness, "Tombo! She's a married woman! Our boss's wife, no less! How on earth could you impress a human woman?"

Tombo winked at the crowd and went through his choreography. Executing a backwards somersault, landing perfectly back in place, and cartwheeling atop the stool. After the last cartwheel, he beat his chest with his fists. Tombo then performed the back flip off of Zeke's head.

The crowd stood to their feet, clapping and shouting elatedly. They began chanting, "Tom-bo! Tom-bo! Tom-bo!"

"That's how." Tombo's lips moved as Zeke dusted off the top of his hat. "How would you impress a woman?"

"Well, what makes you think I want to impress women?" Zeke said.

Tombo's eyes glared at the top of his own forehead, and he settled the backs of his hairy wrists on his narrow hips.

"But—if I needed to impress someone, I have talents."

"Let's see them then," Tombo sassed.

Zeke stepped forward, closer to the audience. He turned his head to the side and smiled in a coy manner, as if he were aiming to impress them. He brought both arms, loosely flexed, in front of his chest and positioned his feet in ballet first position. This brought attention to his red sequined ballet shoes, which sparkled in the spotlight.

Zeke stepped, extended a leg, and began pumping a string of fouetté turns. He increased in speed and pirouetted faster. He then commenced his most impressive ballet moves. A butterfly followed by four double tours. A spin that rolled on his knee from a kneeling position and then back to standing again.

From fourth position, he gracefully turned and leaped into a very high grand jeté, legs perfectly straight and split in mid air. Landing smoothly and gingerly stepping, he circled the stool and stopped to give a humble bow to Tombo.

Again the crowd raved and shouted, "Bravo!" High-pitched whistles of encouragement from spectators rang out and reverberated from the walls of the room. Tombo began clapping and his smile showed all of his teeth as their song about friendship played.

They harmonized the chorus. The audience, now invested in this spectacular form of ventriloquy, searched with eager eyes and wondered how one person could make two different voices at the same time. Faces of bewilderment and awe, fluctuating back and forth like the ebbing of a river.

Their song and act ended with a crescendo and an iconic high five. Zeke held Tombo's small hand as they bowed and moved to exit the ring. Before they had taken many steps, Caroline ran out to meet them and bent down ceremoniously to kiss Tombo on the cheek.

Their act, by far, had gotten the most jubilant response from all spectators; including the Hagans and the Mandevilles. And our little group was thrilled for Zeke and Tombo.

As the center ring cleared, the lights began to fade dimmer and dimmer until they were completely out. Muffled conversation and speculation dispersed in the stands. In pregnant pause, with vision occluded, the smell of cotton candy, popcorn, and hotdogs were heightened. As was the feel of warm body heat from being enclosed in such a multitude. It was almost uncomfortable.

Anxiety mounted in hypothesizing what was coming. No one in the crowd was expecting the next act. No one in the crowd had seen anything quite like it.

Chapter 15

Rockstar and Revelations

In the darkness, a boom reverberated and echoed throughout the room, continuing at a steady count of four-four timing. It came from a long skinny foot hammering a pedal.

Everyone grew quiet. Three rotating lights above the center ring began participating with dark flashes of red. They illuminated on and off with each beat.

A rapid string of high pitched tinging off of cold brass cymbals entered as laser lights danced around the pitch black room in sharp streaks, alternating and creating patterns. After another minute of anticipation, floor lights swept the room in red and blue, showing the audience a first glimpse of what was coming next.

Alex stood behind his set, his sticks pointed up to the ceiling, as he nodded his head with each hammer of the pedal. No shirt, black board shorts, and sweat bands around his wrists. He launched himself in a back tuck, landing in place with his arms extended triumphantly.

He hopped back onto the drum throne, like he was being dropped from the air into place, and twirled his sticks. They spun like nunchucks over his head and in front of his chest. Beginning with a rapid, soft trill on the high tom, he revolved an arm behind his head to hit the cymbal.

The tempo began steadily climbing. When he was satisfied with the build up, he let loose into a raucous thundering of all drumheads, arms flying up and down, crossing and uncrossing in front of him. Louder and louder, spinning his sticks between each strike as he went.

He switched gears again. Slowly and softly, he worked on the glockenspiel as the drum beats kept going. With the tempo increasing again, and double bass pedaling added, jaws dropped across the arena.

A few more strikes and he slowed to a stop. He had the crowd's full attention.

Alex let out a loud guttural war cry of a scream and tore into the beating and slamming of toms, cymbals shattering at full intensity. His foot pounding the pedal of the bass drum. Veins were bulging and sweat was flying in droplets as he thrashed his head. Each of his limbs were operating in a different direction, like octopus tentacles.

The explosion of beats went on for a full minute before stopping. The crowd went wild, standing, clapping, and screaming sounds of approval. Two technicians ran toward the drum set from opposite sides and assisted Alex in strapping into the platform harness. They checked the integrity of the track, platform, and controls. Once they were satisfied, they walked back to the control station as

Alex hyped the crowd, gesticulating to keep up the noise and applause.

The platform began to rise vertically between the tracks. As soon as it was off the ground, Alex counted off a beat with his drum sticks. His face lit up with exhilaration as the coaster climbed. Pacing himself, he played another dynamic solo while traveling up in the air.

The track rose until it cleared the high wire and then began its journey across the room, slowly rising and falling in a wave pattern parallel to the ceiling. Simultaneously, the platform rotated three hundred and sixty degrees as it rode across the wave. This would place Alex completely upside down three times. From overhead and above them, upside down in his harness, he winked at members of the audience while he played.

As he progressed, a slew of dancers poured out onto the floor below him. Their costumes extravagant and choreography synchronized to the well rehearsed drum solo. A pair of fire breathers blew flames up toward him from beneath, a circus' form of pyrotechnics.

Once the platform had crossed the entire room, it locked into a vertical circular track. There he would ride back and forth along the track, like a pirate ship swing boat at a carnival, until he was upside down again at the top of the circle.

Teenage girls watched him from below with stars in their eyes, and little boys thrashed and slammed their imaginary drum sticks. Women fanned themselves, acting like the fire breathers had heated the place up, but I knew better.

I watched Alex at the culminating pinnacle point of his coaster debut, which was electrifying to all. Sure, he was my partner in crime and travel companion for the past few years. And I knew that sometimes when he played I would get a slight shiver down my spine. But seeing him in Merdwick, that first show, was something different.

I felt impressed, awed, allured, and slightly possessive. Not that I could let him know that. So I just peeped from far away at the entry doors, envious of the view that the Hagan's had; really that anyone who bought a ticket and sat in an actual seat had.

"So. Does he know?" Shay's voice made me spin around so fast I felt like I had been caught spying.

"Hmm? Who know what?" I replied.

Shay dropped her chin and looked at me knowingly, "You know my secret. I know yours. Actually, I've known yours. You don't have to be a mind reader to put that together. I just didn't know if we were to a level of friendship to discuss it."

"And we are now?"

"You're avoiding. But yeah, I think so."

"I don't know what he knows. Or what he thinks, I mean. And I'm not planning on figuring it out or asking him about it," I answered her hushed and sharply.

"Well, you've traveled together for more than a year. Without a contractual demand for it. Simply because you both like it. Because you both like doing it together. And he hasn't breathed a word about going his own way," she paused as I processed, "It's easy to see…"

"I don't know." I had to get off the subject so my stomach would settle back down. "We've got stranger things to concentrate on now. Alex's set is almost done. What's the deal with this mermaid?"

Shay knew I was switching gears purposely, which made me feel a little exposed. She knew all the thoughts swirling around in my head. Nevertheless, she kindly obliged me.

"I don't know about the mer-person."

A great roar resounded in the arena. Alex had finished and was exiting the coaster. He threw his sticks like frisbees, out and into the audience. Rock star mode. He was heading our way to exit the arena.

I jumped out of the doorway and acted like I was really interested in Shay's hair. Thankfully Shay played along, pretending everything was normal and we had just been discussing our performance.

"Guys! That was so freakin' awesome!" Alex said. His face was like a kid on Christmas morning.

"You were great! It was an amazing act. I think you may have stolen the show," I said.

"She's right," said Shay. "I've been doing this a while now and I haven't seen an act like that before. The crowd loved it."

"Man, I can't wait for tomorrow. I'll never be able to get enough of that." His eyes floated toward the ceiling and he was momentarily daydreaming about the next ride.

A few thoughtful seconds and he snapped himself back to reality, "And you guys! You guys were great! What the heck happened at the end though?"

"Henry says our rigging must have skipped a track on the pulley system. Should be fixed by tomorrow. But now we're on probation," I said.

"Aw man, Reg got you."

"It's fine, we'll be back in good graces by this time tomorrow," said Shay.

Alex was searching my face for hidden clues regarding whether Shay was right about that. "Alright. Well good." He let it rest.

A big pink blur came sprinting toward us.

"Holy cow! You were amazing!" Ava's effervescent praise resounded and other performers passing by glanced to see what the noise was about. Her eyes glittered as her lashes blinked enthusiastically.

"Thanks, Ava," Alex said with a grin.

"Really, that was incredible. I knew it would be cool, but I have to admit I was a little worried what would happen if you got stuck up there."

"Oh, Reg has had the guys on it. Should be no worries of that."

Shay and I glanced from Alex, to Ava, and back to each other, smiles cemented on our faces.

Ava's eyes were dancing all over the place and I couldn't tell if it was just her usual level of enthusiasm or if she was turning into one of the teenage girls in the audience.

Alex brushed his hair back and wiped some sweat off his brow. His shirtless torso was glistening. I had taken notice and now so had Ava.

Ava looked us up and down. "Girls, are you okay? I was worried sick for a minute."

"We're okay. Shouldn't happen again," Shay answered.

"Your routine was great, Ava," I said. "I loved your part with Eloise."

"Thanks! I love Daniel and Eloise—two happy souls. Glad I get to do that bit with them."

Shay leaned into the circle, "We were just discussing the merperson. Any of you heard anything about it?"

Alex and Ava shook their heads no.

"It's gotta be coming now. We're at the end of the show," Ava guessed.

Chapter 16

Ceto

Inside the arena the dancers were finishing their routine, encouraging crowd engagement just prior to the end of the show. That way the audience left feeling happy, satisfied, and part of the whole experience. Some dancers spun in feather headdresses, others flipped and somersaulted. They parted their colorful formation to make a pathway to the center platform.

Reginald and Caroline strode down the way, between a sea of choreography, glitter, and light. Hand in hand they walked up the steps.

Through his microphone and over the speakers, Reginald's voice boomed, "Ladies and gentlemen, we hope you have enjoyed the show! Thank you for coming out to support Mr. Hagan's cause! The entrepreneurial ingenuity that is Green Vitality, Inc."

The audience intensely applauded as Mr. Hagan stood and waved to all in the room before taking a little bow.

Reg continued, "We want each of you to have experienced a night you will always remember! So, we have one more surprise exhibition for you before the night's end!" He extended his hands toward Mr. Hagan and then bowed to him, attempting to show deference.

Notes rose from the voices of a male choir, but only in wordless tones, ominous and dark. The lighting dimmed.

Though I had not noticed since we had arrived, nor during practice, there was a sliding segment in the ceiling that could be opened. Everyone in the arena followed Reginald's gaze and looked up to the movement above them.

A long case was being lowered down from the roof. Simultaneously, roustabouts rolled the green and silver circus wagon toward the center ring, just five yards from where Mr. Hagan sat.

The process of lowering it felt like ages, and the room was filled with tangible anticipation. Shrouded in purple velvet, the case descended until it sat on the platform within the circus wagon. Roustabouts straightened the velvet sheet and Anthony made his way to the side of the case.

The choir ended in the softest whisper of voices, and one could have heard a pin drop. Children had scooted up, to perch at the edge of their seats, leaning as far forward as they could. Their eyes alternating from wide in wonder to squinting scrutiny.

"Divers flock to this area in search of ship wrecked treasures. Gold doubloons, emeralds and rubies, oyster hidden precious pearls. What we have here is something of a treasure chest," Anthony said. He paused and his eyes scanned the room nervously.

This was about to elicit one of two types of responses in this little sea town. Shock and wonder—mixed with feverish minds deciding just how lucrative this could be, or flat out horror, rioting, and chaos. I thought it was cowardly that Reginald was making Anthony be the bearer of our fate. Since this whole orchestrated mess was his idea.

"What we have here will make history in Merdwick," Anthony continued. "You may have a strong reaction to it."

By this point, the Hagans were edged forward with curious looks on their faces. They glanced behind their giant bench of a chair to gauge the crowd.

"Before we reveal our last surprise, you should know that this case houses something very powerful. Please remain seated and maintain your distance," Anthony cautioned as the roustabouts strung out a barricade of chains in case anyone were drawn to their feet and went near the exhibit.

Reginald stepped forward and took over from there. He had to be sure that he would get the glory. With a look of great self satisfaction, he announced, "Ladies and gentlemen, The Mandevilles' Marvelous Marvels present to you... Ceto!"

After a slight pause, Anthony ripped the fabric off the case and stepped back. Purple velvet swished into the air and then sank to a fast halt, limp and lifeless.

In the water filled plexiglass, long and numerous strands of sea grass swirled around the sandy colored body of Ceto, making it hard to view the creature. A glimpse of its black-spotted dorsal and caudal body was seen moving through shreds of green.

It must have felt jostled by the descent from the ceiling because it was moving a lot more than when Reginald let the troupe view it. It swished its tail fin in great swipes within its small confining tank, knocking it against the sides intermittently.

A webbed hand slapped the side of the case, and the audience on the south end of the room gasped. Ceto was rolling. Its slender body of scales rotated in the tank. The other hand smacked and suctioned to the glass, like an octopus sucker.

Ceto insidiously extended its neck forward through the seaweed near the edge of the glass, unveiling its eerie face. The audience finally viewed Ceto's smooth and ridge topped scalp, cleft nostrils, and protuberant eyes.

The crowd's response varied. Women shrieked, men gasped, noises of all sorts came from the south end of the room.

Ceto jerked and shuddered before rolling one hundred and eighty degrees to the north side. The side where the Hagans sat. Again it suctioned its hands to the glass and slowly brought its head forward. It was then that I realized Ceto was viewing us as much as we were viewing… it.

Initially, its face was as emotionless as I had first seen it, as it surveyed the north side audience. But then something changed. Its dark orbs of sight shimmered in blue sparkles, but its mouth opened wide and angry. Though no one in the room could pinpoint where the creature's vision was fixated, I thought it could only be on Mr. Hagan.

The face of the creature was positioned very close to the glass now and facing the VIP seating where the CEO sat. It began slapping the glass. Great thuds resounded as children squealed in fear. Over and over it hit the side of its plastic prison.

Its body writhed and thrashed about, creating bubbles and swirling up seaweed. The range of movement within the plexiglass was increasing in speed and intensity.

Mr. Hagan's countenance varied from smirk, to caution, to excitement, in a rotating fashion as the creature continued to rage. Reginald scrupulously monitored Mr. Hagan's reactions and after he deemed he was safe, he approached the giant chair where the Hagans sat.

"You've outdone yourself with this one, Mandeville," said Hagan, a grin creeping up the corner of his mouth as he continued to stare at the angry beast.

"I had an idea that you would enjoy our final showcase," said Reg, "a gift to you in exchange for a few shares of Green Vitality."

Mr. Hagan rubbed his chin, "The thing is, this could jeopardize my importation of supply from sea. And I cannot have that. So you're going to take it back to wherever the hell you found it."

Reginald looked confused, "But you can exploit this thing as you see fit."

"And I will. You bring it to the last show and people will buy tickets to your circus hand over fist. You give me fifty percent of tomorrow night's ticket sales and I'll give you some shares," Mr. Hagan said cooly and powerfully. Like he knew the deal was done already. As though, if he didn't get his way, he'd use other means to ensure his company was safe.

"Fifty percent! Come on, Hagan. That's not reasonable."

"You'll give me fifty percent and you'll dump that thing as soon as the show is over tomorrow."

Reginald was growing pink with frustration but knew he had no other option at this point. The goal was to make the deal. He'd just have to take the loss. Surely his shares would exceed whatever money they left on the table tomorrow night.

"You're tough, Mr. Hagan. You are. But for one hundred shares, I'll do it."

Mr. Hagan was in thought, "Persistence. I like that. Ordinarily I'd cut you down to fifty, but I'm going to take a chance on you. I expect a big turn out tomorrow night."

They shook hands vigorously until a loud bang redirected their attention back to the glass case. Ceto was thrashing so hard that the case was jostling on the wagon. Reginald signaled to Anthony, who ran to cover it back up with the velvet sheet.

The movement slowly declined. The room was quiet, and the crowd was blank faced, trying to understand what they had just seen.

"Alright ladies and gentlemen, that's all for tonight!" Reginald strode toward the case and stood before it with his arms extended to the crowd. "If you didn't get enough, we have one more show tomorrow night. Tickets available for sale as you leave! Thank you for attending The Mandevilles' Maaarvelous Maaarvels! And good night!"

Jubilant circus music sounded. Caroline ran to Reginald's side, and they bowed and curtsied before an applauding audience. The masses began filtering out from their rows of seating. They took last glances at the veiled case and walked out the arena into the night air.

Chapter 17

Indebted

As soon as the room cleared, roustabouts began to scurry around checking equipment, cleaning aisle ways, and helping to transport and feed the animals. I went to go talk to Henry and check out our rigging and pulley system myself.

I almost pivoted on my heels and turned around when I saw that Reg was still in the center ring. But it was too late. He had already made eye contact. I had no choice but to put on the most confident face I could muster and continue. He intercepted me about half way to Henry.

"Miss Morgan, just the girl I want to see. I didn't get to finish what I was going to say to you earlier." His brow furrowed, but he wasn't turning pink yet. Which I took as a good sign.

As he scanned my face for reaction, he must have noticed me glancing up at the rigging, and at Henry. "Are you taking initiative to check your own rigging? Well Well Well. It's like you don't want to be stranded here after all."

"No, sir. I want to continue on with the show." I worked to sound flat and unfazed.

"This show has no room for mediocre and weak performers. If Shay had slipped, she's smart enough and strong enough to smooth out the aesthetics. You, on the other hand, are not. And I don't see how that's going to change over night."

"I will not slip tomorrow night," I said, eyeing him. I tried to walk past him, but his big hand pressed my shoulder back.

"Listen, girl. The only reason you have a chance at that is because for some reason my wife showed you compassion. But even she can't save you a second time." He shoved my shoulder and then let me pass, "Have a good night, Miss Morgan. Don't miss the ferry."

I wasn't scared or shook. I was angry. Angry that he could talk to me any way he pleased. Angry that he was right, I wasn't as strong as I could be. Angry that he had the power to wreck my world. To separate me from my new family, from Alex.

I tried to clear it out of my head in the few seconds it took to walk to Henry, who again apologized profusely. I asked him to show me how the system worked, so he and I could both double check it before the act tomorrow night.

When everything was back in order, we walked the pathway through the palmettos to the marina under a brilliantly clear sky. It was full of stars, and a waning gibbous reflected off the surface of the sea. A pleasant ombre beginning with a lighter horizon and growing darker and darker as it rose in the atmosphere.

Staring out into the expanse brought me peace as we waited to board. I was reminded of Whisper. The beauty of the night sky was like a hug for my soul. A reminder that there is so much more beyond today's struggles.

Our group walked across the gangplank and settled near the stern since we were some of the last performers to board. Everyone around me was upbeat and energized. Reeling off a successful show, theorizing about the sea creature in the plexiglass case, and discussing plans to hit up The Old Seawitch when they got back. I just watched the wake bounce off the side of the boat. In a daze until a pair of forearms leaned on the rail in front of me.

"You okay, Dastardly Jane?" Alex asked, in an attempt to inspire some laughter at my pirate name, but also genuinely wondering.

"I'm fine. Wish it hadn't happen that way. But I'm fine." I half smiled before looking back to the wake.

"The act was great. It wasn't your fault. And I'm glad you got back up there. Would have been a nasty fall."

"Yeah, I need to work on my upper body strength I guess." I said it to him nonchalantly, but replayed Reginald's tirade in my mind.

"I was really worried there for a minute. I mean, it only lasted a few seconds, but it felt a lot longer," Alex said, gazing out at the horizon.

He didn't move. I searched his face and posture for signs of emotion, but he remained stoic.

For a second, I felt comforted that he would worry about me. Then I shoved that feeling as far away as possible. This attachment to him, that I was beginning to notice now thanks to Shay and Ava, would not do me any favors. Distance was safer. I had to switch subjects.

"I got Henry to show me the pulley system so I can double check it myself tomorrow night."

"That's good."

We were approaching the docks at Seafarer's Cove. Warm light shone from the windows and entryways of the stone building. It was actually a welcome sight.

"You hungry? Wanna go to the pub?" Alex asked.

"I think I'm just going to chill and try to relax tonight."

"How are you not hungry? I'm starving," he replied.

I shrugged with a smile, "I only expended a fraction of the energy that you did tonight."

We gathered our stuff and walked over another gangplank. It was humid and there was no escaping the smell of salt water, even once we were in the hallway leading to our rooms. But I loved that smell.

"I'll see you in the morning," Alex said cheerfully.

"See you in the morning."

I walked further down the hallway, unlocked the door to my room, flung my stuff on the edge of the bed, and went to the sink to pull rhinestones and sequins off my face. I heard Shay and Ava come in talking and laughing.

"Hey, do we need to keep these facial sequins for tomorrow?" I asked in an odd vocal tone since my lips were almost closed. That way I could tighten my cheek and it wouldn't hurt as bad to rip glue off my skin.

"No," Shay's voice rang, "And baby oil will help get it off. You can use some of mine."

The process of returning my face to normalcy took a good ten minutes. When I came out of the bathroom, the girls were in their nightwear, but their faces were still spackled performance characters.

Shay jumped up saying she called next. As she closed the bathroom door, Ava crossed her arms impatiently.

"Janie, you were really brave tonight. That had to be scary."

"I didn't think I could get my arm back up there. It's kind of a miracle," I said as I turned to face the corner for modesty and changed into normal clothes.

"Tomorrow night will be better. No accidents. Henry is sick over the whole thing. He won't let it happen again," said Ava.

"I thought Reg was gonna fire him."

"Yeah, I think he was going to. But Henry is our only rigging expert. So he got the same ultimatum as you."

"What? Never let it happen again or walk the plank?" I retorted.

"Pretty much. But it won't happen again, so you both will be fine," Ava said encouragingly.

I sat on my bed and faced her. I could see she was on a new train of thought now.

"I think the show was great. Reg should have no complaints. He and Caroline did their thing. Zeke and Daniel were on point. You and Shay didn't die. The creature didn't cause complete mass chaos." She laughed and rolled her eyes. "And man! Alex's act was something tonight, wasn't it? How long has he been drumming?"

"Long time. Since he was a kid. The coaster thing is new," I answered with a laugh.

"It was very impressive. I think the crowd loved it. Especially the women," she tested.

"Drummers have an effect on people."

"I know we've already been through this, but you're telling me it had no effect on you?" Ava asked with a smirk.

I rolled my eyes at her with a smile and flatly said, "No."

"I just don't understand how that's possible. He's cute and talented. You've been around each other this long."

I thought quickly. She was right, and I didn't want to let her know it. Shay and I were close. But Ava and I were not on that level. And Ava talked a lot. A whole lot. So I said the first thing that came to mind.

"He's like a brother to me." As soon as the words left my mouth, I realized how wrong they were.

"You guys don't fight and bicker like siblings," Ava's eyebrow raised.

"We do. You just haven't seen it yet, I guess."

"Okay," Ava said hesitantly, as if she was not satisfied. "Has he ever dated anyone since the two of you started traveling together?"

"Uh—no."

"Interesting. And how do you think you would feel if he did?"

"Ava, I wouldn't care." I was starting to sound defensive.

"Uh huh," Ava responded, her eyes nonchalantly inspecting the ceiling.

"Why are you asking anyway?" I blurted it out but instantly wished I could retract the question. My stomach bubbled with anxiety about how Ava would answer this.

"Well, like I said, he's cute and talented. I room with his best friend. Whom I have determined through interrogation has no romantic ties to him." Ava paused, "Maybe you could see if he's at all interested in me."

The last line out of her mouth poured out like she was talking about the weather. Like maybe he was, maybe he wasn't. As if it really didn't matter, but why not entertain ourselves with the thrill of it all?

I had predicted her answer accurately, but that didn't stop my guts from responding to it. I kept a straight face and busied my hands with my suitcase, but inside it felt like I really did fall off the cube at the circus. Splattered on dusty arena floor.

"Yeah. I'll ask him," I replied. Ava eyed me like a hawk, checking for emotional breaks. I must have kept composure because she started pulling out her magazines.

Shay came out of the bathroom, fresh faced, and told Ava that the sink was all hers.

"I'm going to take a walk around the cove. I'll be back in a little while," I said.

"Alright," Shay replied.

I had to get away from her before she heard what I was thinking. I gave her a fake smile and went out the door.

It was pretty dead in the hallway. I braced my back against the wall outside our door for a second to steady my breathing.

"Could this night get any worse?" I thought in my head. "It feels like everything is crashing all around me."

I walked out the entrance that led to the street The Old Seawitch was off of and marched in the opposite direction. I wanted to get further away from sight, in case any performers noticed the new girl sulking.

I walked along a busted up side walk until I reached the ocean. There were no benches around, so I just sat on the grassy hill. My arms wrapped around my knees, trying to hold myself together physically and mentally.

"Whisper," I searched for where to begin, but then ended up deciding to keep it real, "this sucks. I know you are here, but I feel very much alone."

I looked out at the sea. The sky was still clear, stars and moon aglow and reflecting on the water. A gust of sea breeze whipped my hair. Breathing in, I tasted the salt of it. I tried to focus on the enormity of the earth before me, sky and water.

"I guess I'm hoping for some reassurance," I mumbled. Mindfully relaxing my shoulders and loosening the grip I had around my knees, I listened to the sound of my own breath and thanked Whisper for it. "I'm alive. I'm moving forward. And you are with me. I intend to stay in this circus. No one can stop me, not even Reginald Mandeville. I will keep going." A new mantra.

The cicadas in the longleaf pines and palmettos nearby began to sing. A dark silhouetted heron flew low to the water, almost grazing the surface of it. I put my palms down on the grass beside me and felt the warm earth that held me up. Whisper was working their magic, and I felt comfort. When everyone and everything else had gone or was taken, Whisper remained. I always feel that in my heart, mind, and body.

I knew I would be scared, sad, and agitated again. Maybe as soon as I got up and walked back to my room. But Whisper is always present. Throughout the yin and yang, the emotions that this life constantly brings.

I criss-crossed my legs and rested my hands on my knees, looking out at the faint horizon beneath the moonlight.

"You're a bit far from the cove," came a voice from behind me in questioning tones.

I jolted out of my solitude and spun around as I got to my feet. Was I in trouble again? In the darkness, it took me a few seconds to figure out who I would be talking to.

"Easy," the voice responded.

It was a woman, slender and poised. A shawl hung around her shoulders and fluttered from the gusts of the westerlies. Her blonde hair seemed to glow in the moonlight.

"Oh, Mrs. Mandeville. I'm sorry." I didn't really know what I was apologizing for, which I hate doing. I just reacted from being off guard.

"No need."

"Hey—um—thank you for what you did tonight. For giving me another chance," I stammered.

Caroline took a step forward beside me and looked out over the shadowed water. I turned to look with her. It was awkwardly quiet for a minute, and I was unsure how I should act around her. With Reginald, you mostly just stood at attention like a soldier whenever he came barging through. It was hard to know how to approach or even be around Caroline. She gave off an allure that made you want to trust her, but Shay was adamant when she told me not to.

"I was sixteen when I started performing with Zingo's lot. But I had a mentor, a master contortionist. She taught me everything she knew. We were very close. One night I missed a pose, rolled out of a chin stand during the performance. Zingo was furious. Told me I was done. Planned to kick me out." She turned and looked at me, "I had nowhere else to go. No family to return home to. My mentor, Tati, vouched for me. Got me another chance."

"I guess I can relate," I said, glancing to the ground.

"Tati said that was it, one more chance to prove my worth. She said she wouldn't step in for me again. That I'd have to make my own way. She said this kind of thing builds character, a chance to rise to the occasion… but she also insisted that I owe her."

"I see," I said. "What do I owe you?"

Caroline placed a delicate hand on my shoulder, "I'll let you know when I decide." She gave me a soft pat, smiled, and turned to walk back to the cove.

I watched her graceful departure. Blonde hair swirling, floating on the night breeze.

It took some time to process what had just occurred. What on earth could I do for Caroline?

Still somewhat bewildered, I bid the ocean goodbye and again walked the busted sidewalk path to the cove.

I made my way to the side entrance this time. The straight shot down the hallway that our rooms were on. I would walk the men's side before getting to the crossroad section and passing on to the women's.

I couldn't help myself. Something deep down in me wanted to run into Alex. To tell him the latest obstacle laid in my path compliments of Caroline Mandeville.

Then I thought of Ava. I did not want to discuss that topic tonight.

Chapter 18

With Anthony's Help

I heaved open the heavy door on the side entrance of Seafarer's Cove. The inside of the hallway was bare. Everyone had either turned in or were still at the pub.

The sound of mumbled talking came through the door of the nearest room. In variable tones and inflections, it sounded like several people were inside. I remembered that Anthony's room was somewhere on this end of the hall.

An audible clicking of the doorknob began. Someone was coming out. Call me nosey, but I slowed my pace to see who it was.

The door slowly opened.

"Thank you," Zeke's voice said as he stepped out.

"Goodnight, Mr. Anthony," said another.

Zeke emerged, followed by Tombo. He hesitated when he saw me, frozen in stance. Tombo looked at me with a conversely calm expression as he scratched his leg absentmindedly.

I scanned back and forth from Zeke to Tombo's expressions, and there was a span of silence.

"Ello, Miss Janie," came a voice in an English accent that paired with Tombo's moving lips.

Zeke swatted him with his free hand, his other hand still on Anthony's doorknob.

"Was that? Did you just? What was that you said?" I sputtered.

Zeke and Tombo looked at each other and seemed to have a conversation with their eyes. Zeke wore an expression of apprehension and Tombo a look of hopeful divulgence.

"Janie, would you care to visit us awhile in our room?" Zeke asked.

I eyed the two of them with suspicion, "I guess so."

We trailed down the hallway in a single file line. I thought how funny it must've looked. Zeke leading the way in his typical attire, boiler hat and suspenders. Tombo in his own suspenders, though they were far more flamboyant, coarse black hair swinging with his gait. Myself in shabby lounge wear with my hair piled on top of my head. Like lost boys trailing through Neverland.

Zeke opened the door. As I entered their room, I saw that it was empty. Alex must've still been at the pub. And he must've taken Daniel because he was missing too.

The room was surprisingly well kept for housing three men and a chimpanzee. It even smelled good.

"Nice room," I said nonchalantly.

"Thanks," Zeke said, pulling the door shut behind us. "I've got them trained. A clean room makes a peaceful room. The lavender oil helps."

"I noticed. So, what are we chatting about?"

"Me, of course. I let the cat out of the bag with you," came the English accent. Tombo sat perched on the end of Zeke's bed. He shrugged his furry shoulders as if it were no big deal.

I looked at Zeke, but he was only staring at Tombo. No quiver at his Adam's apple. No frozen smile.

"You're not doing this?" I asked him.

"No. I perform ventriloquy during the show. That's all me. I've had years of practice imitating the English accent. But there's a reason Tombo is so animated and proficient at mouthing the words I say," said Zeke.

"I should say so. I've been fluent in the English language since I was two years old," said Tombo. I looked at him dumbstruck. He continued, "You see, a fire ravaged my home in Tanzabia when I was a wee little thing. My mother didn't make it. But I was removed from the jungle's ashes by Dr. Zuberi."

Zeke chimed in, "Dr. Zuberi was head of the animal research center and shelter I worked for at the time. Brilliant man, pioneered the protocol for teaching pan paniscus the human language. He was born to an English mother and African father, hence the accent you hear out of this guy," Zeke smiled and jerked his thumb playfully at Tombo. He stared off in thought, "And I'm a sucker for accents. Dr. Zuberi was also my first love. It didn't work out, obviously. But I got to adopt Tombo."

Zeke sat on the bed next to Tombo, who wrapped a fuzzy, lanky arm around Zeke's shoulders.

"It's alright, mate. Plenty of other fish in the sea," Tombo said cheerfully. They were both now quiet, staring at me, and awaiting a response.

"Wow… wow," was all I could utter.

"I know it's a bit overwhelming, dear. You'll come around," said Tombo.

"But it must be kept a secret. No one knows," said Zeke.

"Well, Anthony knows," countered Tombo, "the new fish in the sea, perhaps."

I smiled at Zeke inquisitively as he rolled his eyes at Tombo.

"He's being cheeky," said Zeke. "We're just friends."

"So, Alex and Daniel don't know?" I asked.

"Those two are suspicious, but they haven't caught us yet. Like we were sort of caught by you," said Zeke.

In my head, I wondered if Shay knew. If she's been close enough to Zeke to hear his thoughts, which I figured she had, then she would be keeping the secret too. And Zeke would have no idea she knew. Either way, I would not be able to keep her out of my head. So, she would find out sooner or later.

"Do you two ever plan to tell the boys?" I asked.

"Sure, down the road, when the time is right. We're just trying to be careful. A talking chimp is a desirable commodity. It can't get out to the other circus performers because I don't want it to get to the Mandevilles."

"Oy, they'd have me living with 'em for sure," Tombo's accent intensified as he looked around nervously.

"I'm not letting that happen, Tombo and I are family," said Zeke, "in heart most of all, but also in legality. I have papers."

"Yeah, but this lot doesn't play well with others," said Tombo.

I observed the little chimp's anxious face, "I agree with you, Tombo. I'm not quick to trust them either." Looking at both of them I said, "I promise not to tell your secret." It was my loop hole for Shay finding out, telling being speaking, but they didn't need to worry about her. She would never want to hurt or jeopardize their family.

"How did you get Tombo in here? Rather than in the barn with the other animals," I asked Zeke.

"That's all Anthony. After a few interactions we became acquaintances, then as it continued we became friends. I pleaded my case to him. He told Reginald some story about ventriloquy practices with a live animal taking significantly more rehearsal time. That Tombo needed to be with me more often to rehearse and maintain appropriate human like behaviors. Anyway, he sort of bought it and agreed. But Anthony is still wary and told me to stay out of sight as much as possible."

"Thank heavens for Mr. Anthony. It was miserable being housed in the menagerie on the ship. Cold, smelly, and drab. No one to talk to," Tombo said. He shook his head thinking about it.

There was a rustling sound at the door. All three pairs of our eyes got big and wide. How was I going to explain why I was in the boys' room? Zeke jumped up and ran to his suit case.

Alex swung the door open with Daniel trailing in behind him. His laughter subsided as he scanned the room, looking confused.

"Hey guys!" I said cheerfully, as if this wasn't out of the ordinary.

"Hi... Janie. What are you doing here?" Alex questioned.

"She's borrowing some hair gel for tomorrow night," Zeke answered nonchalantly.

This seemed to suffice Alex. His expression softened. "Oh. Well, you came to the right place," he said, slapping Zeke on the shoulder.

Zeke's eyes grew at the unexpected force of the blow. Like Alex was some ogre who didn't know his own strength. He rolled his eyes and huffed, "Boys."

"Right, well got it," I said waving the tube of gel. "I'll see you guys in the morning."

They carried on, talking about the happenings of the pub. Tombo winked at me as I closed the door.

When I got back to my room, the girls were winding down to sleep. I bid them goodnight and laid down in my bed. There had been so much information revealed in the last few hours, and I hadn't had a chance to sort through it all.

I thought about all these wonderful people, or beings rather, now that I included Tombo. They were all so talented. And some were gifted. They had abilities that average people wished for; me included. I couldn't help but feel a little jealous. Mind reading. Talking monkeys. I was barely hanging by a thread in this circus. I wished I had a little magic.

As I lay there analyzing, I decided to file my complaints with Whisper. In silence, I discussed the grievance I had with being a regular girl via inner dialogue. As I rambled on, comparing myself to my new and beloved friends, Whisper began the usual work of patient listening. Somewhere in all of that, I found some clarity.

Most people would think or say that to converse about the nature of the divine as magic would be cavalier and inappropriate. I had never heard anyone describe the nature of God without careful and predictable semantics. It was okay to discuss the supernatural miracles that occurred through God, but 'magic' was like a dirty word.

"Why isn't it okay to say that God is magic?" I thought. There is an energy to the universe. We try to understand it as a being that artfully sculpts every bit of creation, organizes it. Continues to control it, evolve it. A being outside of space and time. We can't touch it or see it. We cannot fully understand it; not even come close.

This being wants to know its creation, communicate with it. Wants us to see the nature of itself and ourself. To understand our unity, not just with itself but with each other. Our shared humanity. This being wants us to know that we are one.

As a personal side note, humans drive me crazy. That's the cynical side of me. After all of my experiences with pain, disappointment, abandonment. After years watching the dark and dirtiness humans are capable of. It gives me pause, humans give me pause.

But a greater being so complicated to understand, engages in the entire human life span from start to finish. The helplessness of a baby, the wonder of a small child, the struggles of adolescence, and the evolved adult.

We all have access to a counsel that we can call on and speak to privately, in our minds. And that counsel can read our minds, just like Shay's gift.

Doesn't this all sound like magic to you? It's is so complex and difficult to process, not unlike the difficulty to process watching a magician disappear.

So, God is magic. Whisper is my magic. My heart is tethered to Whisper, and I can ask for advice or talk through my feelings at any present moment. It's how I decide, seek solace, and frankly, survive.

Sleep followed after my mind had calmed. The night felt short, and the sleep was deep and dreamless. I awoke to rustling house shoes, dragging across the floor, in and out the bathroom. It took me a minute to remember where I was.

"Who's ready for the final Merdwick exposition?" Ava asked sleepily and sarcastically. I squinted through one eye at her, still buried under my covers.

"I can't say that after the first show I'm inclined to stay in Merdwick. What with almost breaking my neck, and embarrassing myself in front of a huge crowd."

"That was just a bad stroke of luck. The universe's way of initiation. Now you've gone through the worst, so everything else will be cake," said Shay.

"You don't think there could be worse things than that? What if I fall to my death and Reginald laughs and applauds?" I huffed.

"Oh Janie, I must be rubbing off on you. Drama queen," Ava smirked.

"It's good for me. Emphasizes my girlishness. Something that never came easily."

"Really," the airy sarcastic remark resonated from Ava's cheerful mouth.

"Well, you can learn it all here." Shay nodded at Ava. "Miss bubblegum wrote the manual."

"It's okay if you're not girly." Ava air quoted the girly word. "There are all sorts of femininity. You have to figure out and flaunt your own. And you've got it, Janie. You just need to learn how to use it."

"What do you mean use it?" I asked.

Shay's eyes got big and rolled as she mumbled, "Here we go," under her breath on her walk back to the bathroom.

"You can use it a number of ways. To allure a person you're attracted to first and for most. But you can also use it to propose an idea or make a case for yourself in the normal day to day."

"She means bat your eyelashes and get your way," Shay interjected from behind the bathroom door. Ava raised an eyebrow as if that was a total lie.

"I couldn't do that. I wouldn't know where to start," I replied.

"You start by demonstrating confidence. Don't let them see your vulnerability. Just pretend you don't care if it happens or not. I realize that is easier said than done, but practice makes perfect," Ava preached.

"And you think I could do that?"

"Absolutely."

"Well, I appreciate the vote of confidence," I said to Ava. I genuinely felt that way, because by now, I saw her as a model female. The encouragement was nice. And I was new to having females be a source of it.

Shay emerged, "She's not wrong. Self-confidence is a big factor for success in all aspects of life. Romantically and otherwise. But I prefer a different plan of action."

"How do you get self confidence?"

"Well, through spirituality, building physical strength, self love. Self love, as in taking care of yourself. Taking time for you. Making decisions that are healthy for you." Shay paused. "And last but not least, by thinking of others. Looking at the big picture and being grateful. Stepping away from the microscope and looking at what's happening around you."

Ava and I sat in thoughtful silence, like two little students listening to a beloved teacher. Processing the profound set of values Shay just listed.

Ava seemed to feel a little corrected but obviously respected Shay's wisdom. Who knows where the wisdom Shay had amassed came from? She had listened to so many thoughts, from all over the world. Like inescapable research on what's truly valuable in life and what's insignificant.

"Kindness is magic," Shay said, winking at me.

"I love that," said Ava.

"You ladies better get to it. That ferry won't wait for us," Shay mothered.

Chapter 19

Back To The Sea

We arrived at the marina, trekked to the fairgrounds, and carried out the routine preparations for the last show in Merdwick.

Shay and I got with Henry to check, re-check, and triple check our rigging and apparatus. He was again profusely apologetic and eager to ensure that everything would be up to immaculate safety standards. But I never held what happened against him.

Shay did all she could to encourage him, and she earnestly abated his fear of another incident. With a side hug, she told him she had been trusting him for years now, and that the track slipping was a freak accident.

We rehearsed the act as Henry controlled the ascent and descent of the cube. No jolting tumbles or drops occurred. And with those concerns at ease, we went about the usual pre-show agenda.

There were three times as many people in line for tickets as the night before when the sun started to set. Word must have gotten out about the sea creature. By nightfall, as the side shows began their exhibition, the full moon was peeking in and out from behind cumulus clouds that moved quickly across the dark sky. There was a mist floating just above the ocean's surface.

Despite the growing volume of circus goers excitedly discussing tonight's show, it felt like an ominous ambience was spreading onto shore from the ocean. My anxiety was so high at the thought of messing up our act again, I felt a little disoriented. I tried my hardest to evoke the self confidence the girl's had encouraged me to fake until I make it. But extra rosin spray to safeguard my grip couldn't hurt.

The first routines were smooth. Ava and the jugglers made no drops, Daniel and Eloise had the audience enamored, and Caroline and Reginald's acts shocked and amazed spectators. Our show time seemed to come much more quickly than the night before.

"We're going to nail it," Shay said encouragingly, as we waited for our cue behind a curtain.

When our song began to play, Shay led in graceful sweeping steps to the aerial cube. I took a deep breath, exhaled with closed eyes, and channeled the poise of a tiger determined to capture its prey. I followed her with a plastered smile across my painted face.

Once again, we took hold of the cube on opposing sides and stepped in circular fashion to initiate a spin. After our cue, Henry hoisted the cube into the air. We floated up smoothly and stepped through the air.

At the peak height, we transitioned between each pose of our routine. I hoped that there were not many repeat viewers in the crowd that witnessed the debacle at the first show.

The audience seemed to be awed at our routine. I did not see anyone looking fearful or scanning Henry's movements near the pulley system. That was a good thing.

I focused on catching glimpses of little girls with twinkles of wonder in their eyes. That's what spoke to me. I may not be the most feminine, and definitely not an alluring vixen, but if I could inspire whimsical fascination that was good enough for me. If little girls would twirl like ballerinas, or practice flips on the monkey bars after seeing my act, my heart would be warm.

My smile grew more genuine as we continued. So did Shay's. As we came to the last transition, I shoved away any reflections of post trauma. Shay tucked and rolled over the bar to a graceful hanging position. This was it.

Another deep breath, eyes closed at exhale. I repeated her movements.

This time the two of us elegantly hung from the bars of the cube as it continued its slow rotation. With straight right legs, bent left knees, and pointed toes, Shay and I posed like the Arabian fillies that pranced in the acts preceding us.

Henry slowly and steadily lowered the cube until we softly stepped in a circle on the ground, just as we had started.

I was elated, relieved, and probably a little euphoric. This wouldn't cause the Mandevilles to stop monitoring my every move for the slightest mis-step, but it was a win for tonight and an authentic boost to my self confidence. Shay and I stepped forward, held hands, and curtsied to the audience before exiting the arena.

"Thank God," I breathed, as soon as we were back in the waiting area.

"It was great! Perfect even! I'm so happy for you," Shay said as she squeezed me tightly. "See, you can do it. No more self doubt."

Zeke and Tombo both gave us a thumbs up as they walked out to start their act.

I felt good, leagues better than I did the first night. Almost like a different person.

Ava and Alex jogged up to us, and I was taken aback when Alex hugged me almost as tight as Shay had.

"Hey, no falls!" he said excitedly as he squeezed.

"Yeah. This is much more fun without the calamity of cheating death and freaking out a crowd," I said as Ava hugged me too.

"I guess so! We need to celebrate at the pub later," Alex said.

"If you don't fall out and break your neck, then you're right. We should."

"*Pffft.*" Alex's face was smug. "I ain't falling."

"Oh, someone's got the big head already," I said, as Ava watched Alex's posture intently.

"No, I just ain't falling. I may go through the first ever documented case of human combustion from thrashing for ten minutes straight," he made a ridiculous face. "But I just can't help myself."

"You better get going. You're almost up," said Ava.

Alex's half grin made an appearance and he fist bumped Ava. Then he slapped me on the shoulder and went to get buckled in the coaster, like I was a bandmate taking a break for his solo.

"How weird is that?" I thought to myself. She gets a fist bump, and I get slapped. What does that mean? I shook my eyebrows free from being drawn into a frown. Ava winked at me as she bounced off to the waiting area.

I watched Alex's act from an obscure spot side stage. It was as epic as the night before. More people meant more boys air-drumming along and more girls melting into puddles in their seats. Lights flashing, sweat flinging, and veins popping; he was in full form. The coaster travelled the track smoothly; thank goodness. I still got nervous watching him hang upside down. And at the end of the set, he flung each drumstick into the stands as the crowd roared and applauded.

Alex and I had made it, him easily and me by the skin of my teeth. We had completed the shows of the first stop and we would get paid tomorrow. Our plan was working. We had sold our talents to the Mandevilles, travelled to a new place, became a family with the other performers we roomed with, and gotten through our first shows. It felt like a weight had lifted. Like this thing could work for us. Take us all the way to Fimaldi Hunu, where we wouldn't have to worry about the Mandevilles' approval.

I knew I was still on probation, but I wanted to let myself have the peaceful feeling. In that moment, when I watched him walk out of the arena, my brain sort of processed it all in a few seconds. It seemed surreal.

The music and lighting shifted and changed, which snapped me back to reality. They were gearing up for the final exhibition of Ceto.

Mr. Hagan was looking extra eager tonight, now that he knew what was to come. No doubt he had amassed this number of spectators through declaration of the mysteries of the sea revealed. His wife, on the other hand, looked apprehensive and sunk back in her seat, making herself as small as possible. It wasn't until now that I noticed they had brought in more fancy chairs, positioned adjacent to his front row throne, which were filled with his top shareholders and their wives. By the looks of it, he knew it was time to show off.

The sliding segment in the ceiling opened, and Reginald gesticulated toward the long case being lowered down from the roof. The roustabouts rolled in the green and silver circus wagon in front of Mr. Hagan and the shareholders.

The case descended until it settled inside the wagon. The edges of the crushed velvet veil slowing their swish and hanging.

Anthony appeared and began the same spiel as the room was quiet. Almost everyone, including the shareholders who were viewing this exposition for the first time, scooted to the edge of their seats, trying to get an optimal view.

Mr. Hagan glanced around smugly. Soaking in the fact that, through his promotion of the show, ticket sales had quadrupled.

Reginald must have been feeling invincible tonight because he halted Anthony from approaching the case for the grand reveal. Instead, he took his place and grasped the velvet shroud in his gloved hand, "Ladies and gentlemen, The Mandevilles' Marvelous Marvels present to you… Ceto."

The music crescendo exploded as Reg ripped off the veil and the room went silent. He extended a hand to display the transparent case housing the creature.

The swirling of seaweed and grasses seemed to move more quickly tonight. Maybe Ceto knew the routine now. Its tan body writhed in the glass this way and that, but it didn't take time to scan and scrutinize what it was seeing. Instead, it flailed about wildly.

Reginald stepped back and attempted to maintain his composure, but I could see the concern in his expression as Ceto slammed its body against the plexiglass walls. He shot Anthony a confused look.

The crowd was growing precautious too. They realized that the music had never started back up, and that the roustabouts were awaiting instruction. Several people had stood to their feet. Mothers had their children by the hand, looking ready to make a fast exit. Again and again Ceto bashed the sides of the case.

"What we have here is a piece of history," Reg tried to re-focus the audience, "a creature of the sea whose powers are not yet fully known."

By this point, everyone could tell something was wrong, performers and spectators alike. The creature's body was a blur of tan and black as it continued pounding on the case. Reg was mid sentence when a loud cracking sound resounded and droplets of water shot up through the top of the case.

The audience shrieked. They had evolved from inquisition to terror. Several families began to quickly side-step across rows and head toward the exit.

Caroline rushed out to the center ring to talk Reginald out of continuing, but he was holding her off.

Hypnotized by the wreckage of the situation before me, I kept stepping closer from side stage to watch.

Mr. Hagan was looking stern, and I watched his lips move. It looked like he was telling Reginald to, "get it out of here."

Another loud crack and a spray of water shot higher into the air toward the high wire, which elicited several screams and a mass exodus from the stands. Mothers and fathers grabbed up their children in their arms and ran out as a webbed hand flopped over the edge of the case.

Another breaking sound and the creature's head had emerged from the top. It turned to face Mr. Hagan and screeched in a blood-curdling scream, its angry face fixed on his as it started making efforts to get out of the plexiglass case.

Mr. Hagan was mid stance, bent at the knees as he was attempting to stand up. But as Ceto's gaze focused on him, he moaned in pain and fell back into his chair. On his VIP throne, Mr. Hagan convulsed from the electrical disturbances to his brain; his wife grasping at him helplessly in efforts to stop it.

Reginald barked at the roustabouts to bring the metal slabs. They scurried frantically in pairs and two men lifted great rusty metal sheets to be placed on the top of Ceto's case. The big cat tamer joined in on the efforts, cracking his whip across Ceto's arms whenever it reached out of the case.

The creature zeroed in on Caroline's horrified countenance. She too crumbled into a ball on the ground.

Watching all of this, I was paralyzed in place. My feet wouldn't move. Everyone around me had ran out while I watched the events unfold, frozen as a stone.

Ceto turned its head quickly and locked its enormous lifeless eyes on mine from ten yards across the room. My vision faded, and I felt a shock run through my body just before I fell to the ground. Images quickly ran across my unconscious mind like bad dreams. Then everything was muffled and blurred as I laid on the floor.

While I was unconscious, the roustabouts slammed the metal slabs over the plexiglass, knocking Ceto back into the water. Henry ran over to aide them in holding the barricade in place. Together the team began rolling the wagon out to the nearest ship launch.

In a psychological fog, I could see a blurred figure over my head and I knew they were lifting me up. My ears were ringing and the voices around me sounded deadened. In my mind, I was trying to process what I had just seen.

It was like a movie of my life in a worst-case scenario. A flash of Reginald screaming at me, being escorted out of my room and to the streets outside Seafarer's Cove. An image of Alex floating up and away from me, his face flat and lifeless. Ava helping Alex get secured in the drum coaster before kissing him good luck, like they had been together for years. Shay telling me I was on my own, and that she done mentoring me. And worst of all, checking into a dusty, grimy, old motel alone. Sitting on the dirty bed comforter, and crying profusely with no one there to console me.

What did that mean? How did Ceto do that, show me that? Was my body okay or was I half dead already?

I was later told that I was out for a good ten minutes. Gradually coming back to was like someone was slowly turning the volume back up on a radio. People were still yelling and screaming, and there was the sound of feet pounding across the floor nearby, all of which made me wince in discomfort at the effect it was having on my already throbbing head.

I felt my shoulders being shaken vigorously, and I consciously tried to lift my eyelids. My vision steadily cleared until I could see Alex's hazel eyes, wide and scanning my face, his dark sweaty hair swishing as he looked me up and down.

"Janie, Janie, thank God!" he said as he helped me sit up. "You okay? Talk to me."

"Yeah. I dunno. I think so. That was weird."

"Yeah, well, worse than weird happened while you were out," he said with a look of apprehensiveness on his face.

"It made me see things. See bad things happening."

"Bad things?" Alex looked at me as if judging every word, expression and movement, "We need to get out of here."

"It happened to Hagan too, didn't it? And Caroline?"

"Something happened to them, yeah. We can swap notes later. Let's go." He pulled me up, threw my arm around his neck, and started leading me out the doors and toward the ferry.

As soon as we got out the door of the building, another onslaught of chaos was waiting for us outside. Noise everywhere. Animals bellowing and screeching, unsettled in the barn nearby. Families yelling and running about, roustabouts shoving through the crowds. But that wasn't the worst of it.

We were nearing the closest boat launch, where the roustabouts were all running to. I could see Reginald frantically jumping around and yelling at the crew to pull the circus wagon out of the water. It was halfway submerged at that point, and since it was such an ornate piece, he no doubt wanted to keep it from being ruined.

Reg ran from the wagon to the swarm of people squatting and sitting in a huddle near the edge of the water. I picked up on the sound of Ava crying. She was sobbing hard and her weeping was guttural.

"What's wrong? What happened?"

Alex's face looked shaken, "Let's get you to the ferry and I'll go find out."

He hurriedly dragged me across the gangplank and sat me on a bench on the inside terminal of the ferry before he said, "Don't move. I'll be right back."

A few people were already on the ferry, but the bulk of our troupe hadn't made it on board yet. Sitting there, my mind flickered in and out of consciousness, like a heavy sleep was pushing down on my eyelids. Try as I might, I couldn't keep them open. I wished Alex would hurry. I wished Shay was here. Every now and then an acquaintance performer would jostle me awake and tell me to try not to fall asleep. They weren't invested in me, there was not a relationship or friendship established with them, but they still displayed a look of concern when they woke me.

The face that roused me up was a familiar one. Zeke, with Tombo positioned close beside him, patted my cheeks and snapped his fingers in front of me.

"Hmm?"

"Janie, you can't sleep. I don't know if you have a concussion or what, but you need to stay awake til we get you checked out," Zeke snapped.

"Ok, I'm trying."

"I don't even know if we're safe in here," he said, scanning the inner terminal.

"What?"

"Now's probably not a good time, but something's happened."

"What? What happened?" I asked, sitting up and trying not to waver.

"Easy." Zeke steadied my shoulders and then looked down at his knees. "They had a time getting Ceto back to the ocean. The roustabouts were rolling the wagon out of the building and Henry went to help. He was pulling the front end, and led the wagon into the sea."

Zeke had gotten quiet. "What happened?" I pressed.

"Anthony says he saw it. He saw Henry pulling the wagon into the ocean to let it go. And then he just froze. The roustabouts yelled at him to pull, and he fell face first in the water."

"Yeah? yeah?" I pushed worriedly.

Zeke wasn't crying, but looked so shaken, lost in his own thoughts. "They heaved the slabs and Ceto swam out. Then they went to pull Henry out of the water. He... He had a," he paused and tried to determine the most appropriate words, "there were these weapons. Like giant urchin spines with a barnacled handle. They were stuck in his throat, stomach, and legs."

I searched Zeke's face. This couldn't be true. Tombo's face drooped in fear and caution, unable to speak around the other people nearby.

"Well, did they get it out? Is he okay?"

"I don't think so," Zeke answered quietly.

"No, no," this couldn't be real, I thought. "What about the others?"

"It was just Henry."

"Ava was down there. And Alex went down there. Are they okay? We've got to go get them."

"They're fine, they sent me to you."

"Where's Shay?"

"She's with them. They're trying to help sort everything out."

I couldn't make sense of it all. This was too much. Someone I knew was likely dead just outside. Someone too young, someone who was helpful and kind to me.

All my friends were out there in potential danger. It was like I was grasping at something to hold onto and couldn't quite get a grip on it. And then everything went black.

Chapter 20

The Mind Sting

When I could finally lift my heavy eyelids, things were a little blurry. If you've ever experienced what it's like to wake up from sleep being unsure of where you are or why you are there, coming back to consciousness was like that. I jostled around under the covers of the bed until Shay's face appeared over me.

"Hey, hey, it's okay. You're at the cove. You're in your bed," she said calmly.

I dropped my head back down to my pillow. Shay paused for a minute to let me process. Tears ran sideways from the corners of my eyes and down to my ears as I began remembering everything that Zeke had told me. "Is everyone safe?"

"Everyone's fine. The whole troupe is back here in their rooms." She disappeared from my line of sight for a second, "I've got you some tea. Let's try to sit you up a while."

The image of Ceto came to the surface of my mind and made my stomach turn. Shay was definitely close enough to hear my inner dialogue distressing about it.

"You really should rest—but if you want to talk about things—" Shay paused.

"I just can't make any sense of this. What happened to us?"

Shay handed me the mug of tea, "Some town council leaders called in a marine biologist who's been studying the area's waters for years. They seemed less surprised than I would have imagined. I guess they've dealt with similar issues before."

"You saw them? Did you hear anything?"

"Yes. The man's name was Skinner, I think. He got there around the time that the wagon was being pulled out of the water. The townspeople swarmed him like flies. He was looking around, shouting, asking if anyone was stung."

"Stung?"

"Apparently it's called a mind sting. The creatures use it to stun attackers mentally and physically so they can flee," Shay said.

"That's what happened to me? And Caroline and Hagan?"

"I think so."

I remembered the freezing vibration I felt throughout my body when Ceto locked eyes with me. "But why didn't Ceto use the mind sting sooner? The first time we all saw it?"

"It has to be direct eye contact," Shay answered.

"What like Medusa?"

A grin emerged from the corner of Shay's mouth, "Sort of. It doesn't work through an artificial medium like plexiglass."

I slouched down on my pillow, thinking how strange my life had become. I would never have believed in something like this before. "It made me see things. Visions," I told her.

"What did you see?" Shay asked.

I slumped back in my bed and let my eyes float to the ceiling, "Sort of like future scenarios. My worst-case scenario right now. Getting kicked off the circus troupe. Being separated from Alex—and worse." I didn't go into detail, but got the feeling she already knew. "Never seeing you again."

"I'm glad you care about me enough to want me to stay in your life," Shay responded with a laugh.

"It's true. I'm attached now. Sorry," I smiled and shrugged playfully. "I just don't understand what it means… I keep racking my brain. Maybe it was an effect of the seizure."

"What did it feel like?" Shay asked.

"It was like a vibration, or a shock, or something. Painful, uncomfortable, dark. I wonder if Caroline is okay. Did you hear anything about her?"

"She's fine. They sent a doctor here to check on both of you. The doctor said Caroline seemed more affected, she was physically closer to Ceto, but all vitals and tests ran were normal. Both of you are physically okay."

"What about mentally? I hope my brain isn't scrambled," I half laughed.

"No worse than before," Shay teased.

After we stopped laughing, I started thinking of Henry again. He was not okay physically. He was gone. And he must've been scared. Shay was eyeing me and knew what I was thinking.

"But it killed Henry," I whispered.

"It wasn't Ceto that killed him. It was the other creatures. Skinner, the biologist, said they are highly communal. That they retaliated. Henry was a victim to us. Ceto was a victim to them." Shay thought for a moment. "They're wild animals. They reacted. There's only one person behind all of this."

I knew she meant Reg. We sat there silently, trying to process a million thoughts at once. We couldn't trust our leader. It could be life or death. The spinning wheels in my mind were exhausting me further.

"Henry is at peace now. However awful an experience it was that he had to endure, it's over," Shay spoke, almost in a whisper. I watched a single tear roll down her cheek. "He was a kind person."

"So what happens now?"

"We're leaving."

"Where are we going?"

"I'm not sure yet. But I know Reginald will have to meet with Mr. Hagan before we go anywhere."

We spent the rest of the night cocooned in our room. Ava must have come in late while we were already sleeping.

In the boys' room nearby, they discussed the events as we had, and mourned the loss of a man so close to their age, who was taken before his time.

They were no doubt trying to slow the adrenaline that had fueled Alex to help move the body. That fueled Zeke to comfort those in need, which included me and the person blaming himself for Henry's death, Anthony.

Anthony was traumatized. He felt responsible because he was in charge of Ceto. My heart broke at the thought of him enduring a sleepless night. We all knew it wasn't his fault, but how could anybody make him see it that way. A person's perspective, a person's truth, is their own. It's hard to sway.

But Anthony would hear the sound of knocking at his door. And he would answer it to find Zeke and Tombo, hand in hand, ready to be watchful sources of comfort through the long night hours.

That night I was scared to fall asleep. Scared of what I might dream.

When we woke in the morning, the first thing I noticed was that Ava was back to her bubbly self. She was acting like nothing had happened.

When we asked her if she was okay she looked at us sternly and said, "I'm fine. Henry was a good guy. Maybe, at one time, I knew that better than most. But there's no sense in dwelling on it. The show must go on."

Shay later told me they had a history, a long time ago. Back when she first joined The Marvels. Regardless, her way of coping was to re-focus.

Around eight in the morning, Anthony began knocking door to door to let all of us know we would meet at The Old Seawitch at nine o'clock to discuss departure. He looked wretched, but he was holding it together.

When I stepped out the door, I found Alex waiting for us. I hugged him as tightly as I could, which took him off guard. But he reciprocated and understood. We said nothing. There was nothing really to say.

I waited as he hugged Ava and Shay too. The lot of us trudged with heavy feet out of the cove and down to the pub.

When we got inside, we took a booth near Zeke, Tombo, and Anthony. I watched the bartender stick his nose in the air at having to allow an animal inside, and to have its own seat no less.

But Reginald was standing near the door with a look to convey that one should only test him if they're prepared for fury hell hath no. His circus was his treasure. He had come around to the value of Zeke and Tombo's act and grew fond of them. So the chimp stayed.

It grew very tense and quickly silent. The heaviness hanging in the dusty, smoky atmosphere was weighing everyone down.

Caroline was present in a booth next to where Reginald stood. Everyone was trying inconspicuously to get a look at her, without Reg catching them. She wore her usual grandiose style of outfit, but she was more pale in the face than usual, and beads of sweat were visible on her forehead and neck.

There were two locals sitting at a table in the back sipping coffee. "Anybody here that is not part of my circus needs to leave now," Reginald's voice boomed.

Timidly the bartender piped up, "You can't run out customers."

"I said get the hell out, right now!" Reginald screamed. He was turning scarlet, and his neck veins made their usual debut. The two men scampered up and walked briskly out the door. Reginald shot a seething glare at the bartender who stepped backwards until he was behind the kitchen doors.

Caroline placed a hand on his from her seat, which only slightly settled him. "Last night did not go as planned," he began, "It was a damn disaster. We all know that. We lost a member of this circus. It was an unforeseeable tragedy."

Several eyes darted all around the room because several people disagreed with the previous statement. Many of us thought the sea creature exhibit was a bad idea. Reginald himself had said it was very dangerous. Looking back now, the tragedy was not so unforeseeable. And Reginald must've picked up on this.

"That creature, that murdered our Henry, retaliated to Hagan. Hagan has oppressed their kind and used them, blackmailed them, to further his company. To increase his ever growing piles of money," Reginald spat.

We all knew Mr. Hagan was a target, but we also knew Reginald was the one who somehow captured one of the merpeople to exploit it for his own lucrative gains. So how was he any different from Hagan? But he continued to vilify him. And what could any of us really do?

"Mr. Hagan is a sleazy little worm, and I loathe the day I agreed to contract with him for his benefit. He's self seeking and vile. He plans to do nothing, provide nothing, as recompense for Henry's death." He paused and took a breath, "We had an agreement that I would obtain one hundred shares in return for fifty percent of last night's ticket sales. But after last night's events, it goes without saying that he did not make me a shareholder. And because he was personally attacked by that creature, he's demanding his percentage of ticket sales or he'll sue me. In which case he will win, and there will be no more Marvelous Marvels."

There was a rumble of whispering and anxious questioning of performers and roustabouts throughout the pub.

"Quiet!" Reginald screamed, almost as startling as he had when the locals did not immediately get up to leave. "That leaves me with no option. Our troupe is a family. And I know this family needs a job. Needs money. Needs to continue on performing. So I must halve your payment for the Merdwick shows."

To my surprise, the troupe grew louder than before. I watched as faces turned, eyebrows narrowed, and men pushed back their chairs and slammed the table.

"Shut up, you ingrates. This is the life you chose. And this is the deal. If you're going to make a fuss about it, there's the door! You're a bunch of nobodies and you won't last a minute without me." He was scarlet again, spit flying from his lips as he shouted vehemently.

As everyone simmered, Caroline attempted to stand up beside him. Reg tried to regain composure.

"For those of you who plan to stay with this troupe, and not ruin the best deal of your lives, listen up! We're leaving this afternoon for our next set of shows," Reginald's face had smoothed eerily. He knew his next words would roll the dice in his favor, finally. "We'll be traveling by zeppelin to the infamous Mr. Kyte."

When the words left his mouth, there was a noticeable change of countenance in those performers who had been traveling with the Mandevilles the longest. Eyes grew wide and people seemed to float upwards from their seats.

We rookies looked around, and then at each other, shrugging our shoulders. I had never ridden in a zeppelin before, or seen one in person for that matter, so that was alluring. But I wondered if the mode of transport excited the veterans or the name of Mr. Kyte.

As usual, I looked at Shay for any indicators of whether the situation was good or bad, but she remained poised and serene.

"We'll perform two weekends of shows in White Cap Peaks. So you'd best prepare for a major change in temperature and climate. Be packed and ready by two o'clock. Meet on the green by the shoreline entrance to the cove. Any complaining gutless morons can stay right here and poison their livers until we've ascended." Reginald ended his speech as he took Caroline by the hand and led her out of the smoky pub.

As soon as they had walked out, there was an audible roar in conversations amongst all of us still seated in the pub.

"How are they going to fit everything on a zeppelin?" asked Alex.

"We will probably take two. One for the humans and one for the animals. We've used them for travel a couple of times since I've been around," Ava answered.

"Okay. And so who is this Mr. Kyte?" I asked. But no one answered in the usual amount of time it takes for a simple question. Alex looked to Ava, and Ava looked to Shay, who was staring at the table in front of her.

"Mr. Kyte owns the mountains in White Cap Peaks. He basically owns everything there, has for years. He's been building the city up to be a tourist attraction and he's eager to expand," Shay answered.

"Sounds better than Merdwick," Alex said.

"Maybe. Mr. Kyte can be a dangerous type of guy. There's a history of accidents occurring around his attractions. He always gets the mayor to report them as such, but rumors in the circus world are that he can be volatile if he doesn't get his way. We need to be very careful."

"So, why would the Mandevilles want to work with him?" I asked.

"I don't know."

A voice from the booth nearby said, "She's right. We need to be careful." Anthony continued, "We're trying to recover from the first accident. We must be very mindful around Mr. Kyte if we want it to be the last."

The air hung heavy with Anthony's words. They came from a deep and negative place of blame and unsteadiness. You could hear it in the tone when he spoke. I worried about his growing depression. The affect it may have on him and our group.

"I need a drink," Ava spoke quickly. "I don't know if it's a happy drink or sad drink. A celebration that the Merdwick stent is over or liquid courage to face whatever we're about to head towards. But I need a drink. What about you, Alex?"

"Sure," he said.

The two of them walked to the drab faced bartender. Ava jumped up on a stool, her skirt only covering half of her thigh. Alex propped his elbows on the bar next to her and held two fingers up in the air. I watched them chat back and forth as they waited on their drinks. When the bartender brought them out, Ava's shoulders shrugged very high for the first sip, then lowered animatedly as if this was the tool for her relaxation. I watched her sling an arm around Alex and her lips move to say, "Thank you."

Their faces were a little too close for my liking. I felt a lump rise in my throat when he patted her on the back. Quickly I busied myself inspecting the integrity of the window beside me, and any movement by wind or sea outside of it. Otherwise, my face would give me away.

"Relax, it's just a drink," Shay whispered, "bought me and you one the other day too."

"Hmm, what?" I feigned confusion, "Oh yeah, no biggie. Of course."

Shay's eyebrow rose before she opened her mouth to change the subject. I cut her off before she could get the words out.

"Ok, fine." I conceded to show emotion. "You don't think she's sort of making a move?"

Shay and I observed their interactions from afar. I thanked God when Daniel approached them and the duo chat became a trio.

"I don't think so. I don't think you need to worry," Shay said.

"She's beautiful, and kind, and talented. Why wouldn't she? Why wouldn't *he*?"

The conversation was halted when our view of the situation was occluded by Zeke, Anthony, and Tombo.

"Can we join you guys?" Zeke gestured to himself and the others. "Clearly they've abandoned you," he said, nodding at Alex and Ava at the bar.

I rolled my eyes, "Course."

Tombo hopped up on the seat next to me. My first thought was that I wished he could speak here. I felt sorry that they had to hide everything. I got the feeling there were lots of things being hidden about these three.

Then I realized Shay was in the seat beside me. My eyes grew wide as I slowly turned to look at her. She raised her eyebrows knowingly as she took a sip of coffee.

Zeke and Anthony watched our interaction, judging that we were communicating without words. Anthony looked so tired from the long night, but a light bulb must have went off in his head because he perked up too, leaving Zeke to be the only one looking confused.

Anthony had been with the circus longer than us rookies. And being the Mandevilles' assistant, he would know all of Reginald's voiced irritations. Including the fact that Shay would know his thoughts and secrets if he got too close to her.

"We may as well share now," Anthony said, lowering his voice.

"What in the world is going on here?" Zeke asked as his eyes jumped to each of our faces.

Shay leaned in and whispered, "We all have secrets here. But I have access to them."

"What?" Zeke asked, bewildered.

"Will you keep my secret, Zeke?"

"Yes," he answered slowly, with dubious apprehension.

"I can hear other people's thoughts."

"You can?"

"She gave your secret away," she said, jerking a thumb at me and then winking at Tombo. I winced apologetically.

Zeke was computing all that was said. He looked at Anthony and then back at Shay. "Well then. Can you keep my secrets too, please?"

"Secrets? With an s? More than one?" I asked. Everyone stared blankly and hesitantly. "Aw man, now I'm the only one out of the loop."

Zeke looked at me and placed a hand on Anthony's shoulder. "It's new. We don't want to make a fuss." Then, for the first time since the accident, a smile spread across Anthony's face.

"That makes me happy," I replied. And I was truly delighted for them, but inside I felt that all this flirtatiousness was starting to get to me. "I guess everyone is just pairing off," I added, staring at the bar.

Zeke stared, confused again, "Ava and Daniel?"

Everyone laughed. Daniel was looking at Ava with stars in his eyes and had wedged his way between her and Alex. I needed the laughter, I had been in a drought of it for several days now. We all needed it. Laughing together felt like home, felt like family.

"Don't underestimate Daniel's charm," I said to Zeke as I stood up. "I guess I better start packing." I patted Tombo's shoulder and then headed back to the cove. I wanted a moment near the shoreline to myself. To process.

Our time in Merdwick was nearing an end, and by the sounds of it, more treacherous adventures were to come. By two o'clock, giant metal cylinders would arrive to take us away, to a place I'd never been. We would float from warm and humid air, saw palmettos, salt water, and unpredictable sea creatures to something cold and apparently dangerous. I didn't know what to expect. I only knew I was with the right people.

Continue The Series ....

KALEIDOSCOPE
KYTE'S

After a quick escape from the disaster of the last Merdwick show, Janie and Alex find themselves traveling to a new destination. One that is much colder, and not just in temperature alone. The harsh climate is home to an amusement park owned by an entertainment tycoon named Mr. Kyte. And when it comes to prestige, greed, and power, he might give Reginald Mandeville a run for his money.

The Marvelous Marvels quickly discover the new master of ceremonies is a ruthless businessman who loves to up the ante with his circus acts. He knows how to work a crowd, and his demands of performers put their safety at risk. The troupe must band together to endure the unique yet hazardous showmanship Mr. Kyte expects of them.

On top of that, Janie finds herself indebted to Mrs. Mandeville after a mishap during her first Marvelous Marvels performance. She will have to rely on her new friendship with Shay to carry out the task of paying Caroline an owed favor. All while dodging the antics of Mr. Kyte, avoiding Reginald, and navigating her feelings about Alex.

About The Author

J.E. Miller is the author of the captivating fantasy series The Marvelous Marvels. Her books have reached fantasy readers across the globe.

Miller has always had an affinity for the stories that imprint themselves on our hearts and change us forever. She is inspired by the ones that teach us how to grow and serve as a measuring stick for the genuine character we aspire to have.

To find out more, visit jemillerbooks.com or follow @jemillerbooks on TikTok, YouTube, & Instagram.

www.ingramcontent.com/pod-product-compliance
Lightning Source LLC
Chambersburg PA
CBHW021126190726
48288CB00008B/2515